SHOWDOWN

"Just to show you how bighearted I am, I'll give you your choice."

Both of Gardner's guns were leveled at Neil Ashton.

"What choice," Ashton said tightly.

"You can take a slug in the stomach or you can jump." Gardner smiled. "I never seen a man take a two-hundred-foot jump off a cliff. It might be worth seeing."

Neil stared at the gunman. "I'm not going to make it easy for you," he said slowly. "You'll have to shoot."

Renegade Brand

Richard Brister

AVON
PUBLISHERS OF BARD, CAMELOT, DISCUS, EQUINOX AND FLARE BOOKS

RENEGADE BRAND is an original publication of
Avon Books.

AVON BOOKS
A division of
The Hearst Corporation
959 Eighth Avenue
New York, New York 10019

First Avon Printing, August, 1964.
Third Printing.

Printed in the U.S.A.

FOR GRANDMOM

Chapter One

NEIL ASHTON had the feeling that someone was watching him as he idled along. He gave the rimrock hills toward which he rode a careful inspection.

One spot in particular caught and held his attention. It was high, and beautifully screened off from below by craggy upthrusts of granite, an ideal position from which to spot anyone riding southward into this part of the country.

Neil saw a lone rider swing out from behind the granite bulwark and put his horse, a big black, down a steep grade between stunted jack pines.

The man rattled off along a dirt road that would, if Neil remembered correctly, lead eventually into Piperock. Neil knew the man had been spying on him, watching out for his arrival in this Bench country.

He sat debating a moment, consulting his six-year-old knowledge of the topography of this land, then touched spurs to the gray horse.

What followed then was a cross-country ride that refused every opportunity to take the easy way around, that insisted stubbornly on the shortest way to his objective.

A half hour of rugged, up-and-down going brought him out on the dirt road to Piperock, but closer to the town. Neil let the gray horse blow in the shade of a pine, built a brown paper cigarette, and had smoked it halfway down when the rider came along the road toward him, traveling at a relaxed, easy lope.

Neil didn't move. He had a cat's trick of relaxation, his limp body seeming to flow and blend with the gray horse. He had a cat's trick, too, of striking out with bewildering swiftness when a situation called for action.

Crow's feet puckered the skin around his eyes and at the corners of his wide mouth, indicating a man who smiled

7

easily and often, but the eyes themselves were a hard gray, with something haunted looking out from them. His skin was burned mahogany brown by the two weeks' ride that lay behind him.

"Hello, Wes," he drawled as the rider neared him.

Wes Benedict reined in his big black. He was a bony man dressed in a grimy calico shirt, scuffed boots, and faded denim Levis. He was about Neil's age, twenty-five.

Neil was remembering Wes Benedict as the man had been six years ago, a gangling, pimple-faced groom in Piperock's livery stable. The height of Benedict's ambition in those days had been to ride for some cow outfit. He was dressed in puncher's clothes now, so Neil supposed he had realized his ambition.

"What outfit're you ridin' for, Wes?"

"Why?"

"I'd kind of like to know who staked you out up on the rim," Neil said. "It's flattering, of course, considering how long I've been out of this country, but I'm not sure I like being kept such close tabs on."

"I don't know what you're talking about," Wes Benedict said.

"That's pretty much horse you're riding," Neil murmured. "Don't like to renew acquaintance by calling you a liar after six years, Wes, but I'm pretty sure that's the horse. I couldn't make you out, of course. Not at that distance. But that sure does look like the horse."

Benedict sat there gripping the horn, staring at him over the head of the black gelding. The man's mouth was drawn fine. His eyes were sullen, defiant.

"You riding into town, Wes?" Neil grinned. "I'll ride along, if it's all right with you."

"I'm in a hurry," Wes Benedict snapped. He put the big black gelding several steps along the road.

"That's friendly," Neil said, without visible anger.

"What sort of welcome home did you expect?" Benedict growled. He put spurs to his horse, and Neil watched the man disappear around a bend in the road.

Benedict's question echoed within Neil's brain, and his face darkened. He hadn't expected a warm welcome home.

8

There'd been a streak of wilderness in him before he left this country, six years ago. He had done more carousing, fighting, gambling, and general hell-raising than any nineteen-year-old could hope to pass off as mere youthful high spirits.

He knew that his escapades could hardly have endeared him to the good people of Piperock. Nor would the record he had compiled up north add much to his reputation.

There were chapters in his life he would gladly have torn out of the book. He would have liked, if he could, to forget that he had killed a man, and that he had spent time in prison under suspicion of rustling, although he felt no shame within himself at the way those things had come to happen.

He had never considered that his having grown up out on Stirrup ranch, as the unloved, unwanted charge of a vile-tempered stepmother, had in any way shaped him. It was his belief that a man, if he is strong, can give his own life its direction.

During the past year up north he had been in business for himself, trading in horses, and he had settled down, sobered. And then two weeks ago he had received the letter from the lawyer in Piperock, saying that his stepmother was dead, and that Stirrup ranch, under the terms of his long-dead father's will, was now his.

Neil had sold out up north and started the long ride south, retracing the route he had traveled in the opposite direction six years before, when he and his stepmother had finally quit even trying to pretend they could live amicably under one roof.

Now, riding along at a leisurely pace toward Piperock, he told himself that he must make people hereabouts see the change in him. He must win this range's trust and respect, if he was to carve out a niche for himself here as a rancher.

That was his dream, to carry on at Stirrup as his father must have hoped he would do one day. It was a dream he had carried with him almost all his life, a dream that appeared to be coming true.

But remembering his talk with Wes Benedict, he frowned. He felt a queasy uncertainty about the future.

Who put him on that rim? Neil wondered. Who cares that much about the time I show up?

It bothered him that he had no answer. It was still bothering him a half hour later as he sat in a musty law office listening to Horace Pettingill, a dried-up, bespectacled little man with a New England twang.

"As I say," Pettingill said, "there's the ranch, and some cash. Not much. She had her debts. And after funeral expenses—"

"How much cash?" Neil asked.

"Two or three thousand." The lawyer had a disconcerting habit of cracking his knobby knuckles. He cracked them now as he added, "Have you decided what you're going to do with the ranch? I might put you in the way of a buyer. Might even make you an offer myself. As a speculation, of course. I'm no cattleman, Ashton."

The lawyer smiled, showing sharp small teeth, stained and uneven. Neil eyed the man, reminded somehow of an aging ferret, and said quietly, almost disinterestedly, "Why should I want to sell Stirrup?"

"Are you interested in hearing my offer?" parried the lawyer. "I'm no man to dicker. I'll name my top price. After that it's entirely your decision."

"Might be interesting," Neil admitted, "to know what you think Stirrup's worth."

"Twenty thousand." The lawyer was watching Neil's face. Neil gave the man a glance that had nothing readable in it, and indicated the scatter of papers on the desk.

"How long will it take to clean up these tag ends?"

"It depends. A few weeks, if we're lucky. Why?"

Neil pursed his lips, nodding at the bald man. He stood up deliberately now, and moved toward the door.

Pettingill said, a trifle too eagerly, "What about that offer I—"

"It was interesting," Neil said, grinning, and he stepped out onto the boardwalk.

The gray horse was waiting, and Neil climbed to the saddle and swung along the street. As he rode he cast almost no shadow under the noon sun. In tribute to this day's stifling heat, the whole of Piperock seemed to have taken to cover.

Unless, Neil thought, his mouth quirking, the town had taken this way of extending the unwelcome mat for him.

Happy Jack's saloon, on the corner at Main Street and Second, was unchanged, Neil saw, glancing toward the low, ornate building. A half-dozen horses stood switching flies at the battered, badly chewed tie rail. They all wore the Broken Bit brand. Frank Buckmaster's iron. Neil studied the ponies, an old animosity flaring up within him.

As he neared the saloon, a big man with a gristle-hard body shouldered his way out through the swing doors and flung up a huge rope-burned hand.

"Hold on a minute, Neil," he said curtly. "I want a word with you."

Other men were sifting from the saloon, dropping into position around the big man. One of them was Wes Benedict, and Neil eyed him in a purse-lipped silence, thinking that one piece of the puzzle was fitting into place now.

"Your manners haven't improved much in six years, Frank," he murmured. It was a good-natured dig, but Frank Buckmaster's eyes went hard and his craggy jaw stiffened.

"Neil," he said, "I'm not going to put up with the lip from you that I used to."

Neil's eyebrows lifted. Six years, very obviously, had made no change whatever in Frank. This big, enormously powerful man had grown up as heir apparent to a sizable ranch, in a country where cattlemen cast long shadows. As a youngster Frank had been encouraged in an attitude of princely arrogance. Both Frank's parents were dead now, but Frank's insufferable self-assurance lived on, a monument to their folly.

"Now that you're back," Frank said, "what are you planning to do about Stirrup?"

"Why?" Neil asked, frowning a little.

"Stirrup borders my Broken Bit grass. I hear you and some of that bunch you were running with up around Sheridan were jailed and damn near strung up for rustling."

11

Neil took a moment to consider Frank's statement. He swung a leg over the horn, slid down, and stepped up onto the planks, facing Frank. He was an inch or two shorter than Frank, and he hadn't Frank's bulk, but he did not hesitate now.

"What are you saying, Frank?" he asked. "That I'd steal your cattle?"

"I don't see any need to mince words." There was a faint, smiling contempt in Frank's eyes.

Neil hit him a wicked uppercut, catching him squarely on his agressive cleft chin.

Frank had not been expecting the punch. He was driven back against the iron grille protecting one of Happy Jack's windows.

Neil was after him like a dog. He managed to get in three more wicked, lightning-quick blows—one to Frank's gristly midsection, one to the ear, and one to the nose—while Frank staggered backward, off balance.

Frank brought a knee up into Neil's groin. Neil stepped back, grimacing, crippled by the blinding pain for an instant. Three of Frank's men leaped at him from behind. They kicked his legs out from under him and pinned his arms.

Frank had steadied himself now. He stepped away from the building. He had balled his right hand into a massive fist, and cocked the arm for a punch. Neil stared at him, refusing to cringe.

Anger danced in Frank's narrowed eyes, but it was the cold, dispassionate anger of a man in control of a situation. Frank's head moved slightly, and the four men holding Neil, one of whom was Wes Benedict, hauled him up onto his toes and turkey-walked him into the saloon.

Frank followed with the rest of his men. And now, watching Neil, Frank seemed to speculate on the defiance in Neil's eyes.

"Neil," he said, nodding toward a top-heavy-looking man with coppery skin and a straight, vicious mouth, "I don't think you've met Johnny Winema."

Neil glanced at the man, but made no other acknowledgment of the introduction.

Frank's twisted, sadistic smile flickered. "Go to work, Johnny," he said.

Chapter Two

THE COPPER-SKINNED MAN smiled, showing tobacco-stained teeth, and pushed greasy hair away from one of his eyes. He came across the sawdusted floor, still smiling, too happy about this, and yanked Neil's hat down over his eyes.

He went to work on Neil then in a thoroughly business-like way, driving short, ripping punches into Neil's body.

Neil tried to set his muscles against the blows. He struggled violently in an effort to wrench away from the four men who held him. They were old hands at this sort of thing. They held him securely.

This man Winema was a butcher who liked his trade, and knew every trick of it. The man's fists piled into Neil's body again and again. At the end of a minute, although there wasn't a mark visible on him, Neil was retching and gasping for breath.

He was sure a couple of his ribs must be broken. He tried to kick at his unseen tormentor, but the men holding him wedged their legs between his and yanked his arms up behind him. There was a callousness in the way they applied the pressure that made Neil quit struggling.

He stood there and sopped up punishment for another minute. He was wondering how much of this a man's insides could take without permanent damage when a voice, coming from the direction of the door, said, "That'll be all for today, Winema."

The voice had a ring of authority. Winema knocked off the treatment. Neil shook himself free of Frank's men, who seemed willing enough to let him go now, and yanked his hat up off his eyes.

Roy Millership, Piperock's marshal, stood just inside the

swing doors. Frank eyed him angrily and said, "This doesn't concern you, Roy."

"I'll be the judge of that," Millership said. He was about forty, not impressive to look at. A skinny man with a wedge face and enormous ears. A jockey-sized man. But watching him, Neil couldn't help thinking that the marshal packed weight enough for several men in his dark, steely eyes.

Millership glanced toward him, murmuring, "You all right?" and Neil nodded, refusing to give Frank the satisfaction of knowing Winema's punches had hurt him.

"There will be another time for us, friend," Neil told the copper-skinned man.

Again Winema wiped hair off his forehead, and he grinned. The grin was genuine, Neil saw. The man was not worried.

Frank's steady gaze made itself felt now, and Neil looked at the big man. Frank said, "I'd better lay it out for you, Neil. There's no room for your kind up there on the Bench. There's no room for you around Piperock. Realize what you can get out of Stirrup and shake dust on this part of the country."

It was hard, Neil found, not to gape at the man. Frank's hatred of him, he supposed, was instinctive. It went back a long way, to the bloody fist fights when they had been youngsters attending the same one-room school here in Piperock.

One day their natural antipathy for each other would lead to gunplay, Neil supposed, if he stayed around here. The feeling between them went deep enough for that. But somehow this flat order to liquidate and leave the country was stronger medicine than Neil had expected.

"You hear what I said?" Frank asked.

"I heard you, Frank," Neil murmured.

"Well?"

You're too anxious, Neil thought, and he eyed Frank, wondering about that. It was some time before he spoke. "I always take my time on any important decision."

He gave Frank a brief mocking glance, then turned his back and pushed out through the swing doors.

Frank stood for a moment watching the doors slap at each other. When they quit jiggling back and forth on their loose hinges, Frank pivoted toward the marshal.

"Don't let that badge of yours go to your head, Roy."

"Been wearing it," Millership said, "going on ten years. My hat size hasn't changed any in that time." He gave Frank a look that was neither hostile nor friendly, and went out.

Frank shrugged, a gesture of contempt for the marshal that was not, he knew, entirely honest. He grinned around at his riders.

"Wait here," he said. He left the saloon, turning upstreet, making the duck boards resound with his heavy stride. It took him only seconds to reach Horace Pettingill's office. He walked in without knocking, his nose crinkling at the musty odor of Pettingill's lawbooks.

"Well?" Frank said, straddling a chair and pulling a cigar from his pocket. "Did you broach it to him?"

Pettingill nodded. "I broached it."

"How'd he react?"

"He didn't, Frank," Pettingill said. He frowned. "I had the feeling he was laughing up his sleeve at me."

Frank's expression went flat. "He won't be laughing when I'm finished with him. He's already had a taste of what to expect if he wants to be stubborn about this."

Pettingill glanced at his liver-spotted, pale hands. "He looks like a tough nut to me, Frank. And he's quick. He smelled something queer on the wind, if you ask me. Where'd he get that suspicious streak from?"

"You knew his stepmother," Frank said. His grin was an insult to the memory of Belle Ashton. "If you'd had that to grow up with, you'd be suspicious of people too, Horace."

The lawyer nodded, a faint distaste touching his mouth. He said, "Why is it so important to add Ashton's grass to what you've already got, Frank? You're doing all right. Broken Bit's a big outfit."

Frank worked the cigar around in his mouth. "It's not grass I'm after. It's water."

"You've never had any water problem at Broken Bit." The lawyer frowned.

Frank nodded. "Neil and I, between us, control all the really dependable water up there on the Bench, Horace. My creek's never quite run dry, and that spring-fed lake at Stirrup is droughtproof."

"So?"

"Here's a little item of local history you may not know about, Horace, you bein' sort of a Johnny-come-lately around here. Years ago, when the first dry hit this country, Neil's old man threw Stirrup's lake open to all the Bench cattle. He started a kind of tradition. It's been going on so long now that people don't think about it, just take it for granted Stirrup water'll be there, available to their cattle, no matter who's running things up there."

"You've never had to avail yourself of the lake water, I take it?" said the lawyer, and Frank nodded. "I have a notion you'd be less generous with that water, Frank, if you owned Stirrup."

"Damned right. I'd have some of these would-be cattle barons around here crawling to me on their knees, eating out of the palm of my hand." Frank's grin was frankly malicious.

Pettingill sat stroking his chin. "Ranch properties hereabouts will certainly depreciate in value, Frank, once you control Stirrup water." His sly grin flickered. "You wouldn't be thinking of buying the competition out, ranch by ranch, would you?"

"First," Frank announced smugly, "I'm going to whip this range to submission. Then I'm going to own it. All of it."

"I admire your gall, Frank," Pettingill said with a smile.

Frank acknowledged it with a lordly nod. This country belonged, as he saw it, to men with initiative, ambition, to men who dreamed big dreams and laughed at scruples.

"I've had this thing worked out in my mind for years. All I've been waiting for was the right time to make a move. It's here, thanks to Neil Ashton. Who's going to raise any fuss, Horace, if I have to rough him up in order to nudge him off Stirrup? Considering the name he's made for himself up north, that is."

Pettingill frowned. "You won't nudge him off that ranch

16

witout a fight, Frank. That was a generous offer you authorized me to make him. He didn't seem to think much of it."

Frank had lit his cigar. He blew a smoke ring at the ceiling. "He'll think more of it," he said, his voice pinching out the words.

Some of the wicked emotion he felt communicated itself to the lawyer, who swallowed uncomfortably and averted his eyes.

Neil emerged from the barbershop and discovered Roy Millership waiting outside, lounging against the front of the building, cleaning his nails with a jackknife. The skinny town marshal snapped the blade, returned the knife to his pocket, and looked Neil up and down. He cocked his head in mock admiration, murmuring, "Wonderful what an hour in there will do for a man."

"I smell better, too." Neil grinned. There had to be, as he saw it, a reason for Millership's presence here, and after a moment the skinny man got around to it.

"What started that thing up in Jack's place, Neil?"

Neil hesitated. "Why?"

"I think I've earned the right to ask," Millership said.

"Frank as much as called me a cow thief," Neil told him.

"Are you?" Millership asked. Neil frowned, and Millership said, "I've got a right to ask that too, if you and Frank are going to pick up where you left off six years ago."

"Would you believe me," Neil asked, "if I told you my only crime up north was the company I was keeping? That the basis for that charge of rustling against me was that I was seen too much with known rustlers?"

"I might," Millership said. He eyed Neil. "You ran pretty wild that last year before you cleared out of these parts. Seemed like you never hit town without creating some fool ruckus or other." The skinny man's smile was admiring, rueful. "For a while there you made me step lively. You never lied to me, as I remember."

"Thanks."

Millership gave a curt shake of his head. "Don't thank me. And don't expect me to side you against Frank. My

17

job is keeping the peace in this town. I'll keep it, but that's all."

"Fair enough," Neil said. He wished there were some way to get it across to this little man that that wildness was a thing of the past. But you don't convince a man you've turned over a new leaf by talking about it. Neil stared along the street, watching heat devils dance, and pointedly changed the subject.

"I understand Ruth Orr's still in town, running some kind of a boardinghouse for railroad workers. Is that right, Roy?"

"That's right. Her father got jammed between a couple of cattle cars about this time last year. Wasn't much left of him to bury, poor devil. But Ruth's come through the fire jim-dandy. Serves the best meals in town. Everyone knows it. Hasn't had a vacancy at her place since she opened."

"Where is it, exactly?"

Millership's eyes came up, and he frowned. "Neil, there's nothing you can do for that girl except complicate her life for her. She's been through a lot this past year. Why don't you do her a favor and keep away from her?"

"I can find out from somebody else, Roy," Neil pointed out mildly, and he grinned at the marshal.

"The old Turlock place," Millership grumbled, "on Third Street."

The old Turlock place, Neil saw as he turned down Third Street, had lost none of its stately dignity during his absence from Piperock. A man and a girl occupied twin wicker rocking chairs on the porch. Neil had to look twice at the girl before he could be sure it was Ruth Orr. With recognition came a quick warmth.

"Hi, Ruth," he called out as he let himself in through the low wire gate, and he saw that this was a little too casual a greeting to suit Ruth's companion. The man threw a frown at him.

Ruth laughed, a low, pleasant sound that folded the years back. "Typical greeting," she said, "from a man who's been gone six years. . . . Neil, I don't believe you've met Peyt English."

Neil climbed the porch steps and put out his hand. Peyt

English accepted it, but Neil sensed that this stocky, expensively dressed, strikingly handsome man would have preferred to bypass the handshake.

It made him wonder how bad his reputation was in this town. He was careful, for Ruth's sake, to keep any hint of what he felt from showing.

Ruth was saying, in an effort to spark conversation, "Peyt's taken over the old Herber place out on Sunk Creek, Neil."

"That's good grass out there, English," Neil said, smiling agreeably at the fellow. "How's the creek running this summer?"

"Dry," English said bitterly, and Neil frowned. Come to think of it, what little grass he had passed on his way into the country this morning had had a tired look to it. He didn't like to think of the Sunk running low so early in the summer. Now that he had inherited Stirrup, the possibility of a drought took on a special significance for him.

He would have discussed it, one ranching man to another, with Peyt English, but all English wanted, apparently, was to get away gracefully. The man excused himself, murmuring something about an errand uptown, and then Ruth was saying, with that friendliness Neil remembered, "Come see my kitchen, Neil. Pot's on," she added, smiling to let him know she hadn't forgotten he liked his coffee.

She turned into the house, a tall, softly rounded girl whose beauty was enhanced by the unfailing pleasantness of her expression. It was that cheerfulness in her that Neil had always admired, for he knew Ruth's background. At fourteen, she'd lost her mother, and had fallen heir to the task of cooking and cleaning house for her father.

"I didn't hear about your dad," Neil said gravely, "until a few minutes ago, Ruth."

That was all he said. He let his eyes say the rest of it, and Ruth nodded.

"I'm over it, almost," she said. A shadow darkened the blue of her eyes. "He was a wonderful man, Neil. He never earned much with the railroad, but he left me enough in cash and insurance to buy this place and make myself independent."

"What's it like being a landlady?"

"Fine."

"Isn't the work hard?"

"It's just cooking and cleaning. I always liked cooking."

"I know." Neil grinned, and he half shut his eyes, remembering some of Ruth's picnic lunches he'd eaten during his final few months at Stirrup. "I saw Frank a while ago, Ruth, up on Main Street."

"Oh?"

Neil told her what had happened. "He'll try to shove me off Stirrup," he murmured, "if I stick around."

Ruth turned to look at him. "Are you going to stick around?"

"Depends some on you," Neil said, looking into her eyes.

"On me?"

"You told me you loved me once, Ruth," Neil said, very gently, and his gaze remained on hers.

Ruth's coffee was boiling. She lifted the pot off the stove and brought it over to the table. She poured for both of them, and sat down then, and Neil saw the gravity in her eyes.

"Neil, are you daft? Six years ago, when you rode out of Piperock, you rode out of my life."

"I was an irresponsible kid," Neil said, frowning at the memory of what he had been. "I didn't have anything to offer you then, Ruth. I've got Stirrup now. If I thought you and I could pick up the pieces—"

"Time doesn't stand still," Ruth said, and her slow headshake seemed faintly bitter. "Things change."

"Is my reputation worrying you, Ruth?" Neil asked slowly.

"No. But as a friend I'd like to hear your version of the last six years," Ruth admitted. "There've been some ugly rumors. . . . Did you deal faro in a saloon?"

"I dealt a straight game, Ruth," Neil said quietly.

"They say you killed a man."

"He called me a cheat, Ruth, and a liar when I denied it. He went for his gun before I did."

20

There was no guilt, no defensiveness in his manner, and Ruth seemed satisfied with the explanation. She was staring down into her cup.

"Were you really mixed up with a gang of outlaws led by those—those McPhall brothers who were hanged last September?"

"I knew them," Neil said matter-of-factly.

"Frank's been saying you got to know them by selling them horses. Fast horses, Neil, that could be counted on to outrun a posse."

"I worked for a horse dealer in Sheridan, Ruth," Neil said patiently. "It was my job to sell horses. When a man came in for a horse I sold him a horse. I didn't ask questions. Later, when I went into the business in a small way on my own, I sold some horses to the McPhalls. What's wrong with that?"

Ruth smiled ruefully. "Neil, I'm not passing judgment. I just wanted you to know the construction Frank's putting on it."

He felt a quick pleasure at her interest in him. There was an intimacy in what they were doing, sitting here sipping coffee across the small table from each other, that canceled out the six years' separation. Neil looked at her, wondering if she were affected by their nearness, their aloneness, as he was.

He rose without warning, rounding the table, and grasped Ruth at the elbow, lifting her to her feet gently. Her blue eyes were startled as he drew her into his arms. He kissed her, tenderly, experimentally at first.

The touch of her body, the sweet taste of her mouth, roused an old hunger within him, and he crushed his lips against hers forcibly, rudely. He had to know, suddenly, whether or not his kiss could stir her as it had done in the old days.

For an all too brief instant Ruth gave herself freely to his embrace. Then she made a murmuring little protest and tried to push him away.

Neil held her more tightly. But trying to hold Ruth now, he discovered, was like trying to hold a frightened kitten.

21

She twisted out of his arms and stepped back, breathing hard, her generous breasts heaving.

"I shouldn't have permitted that, Neil," she said.

"Why not?"

She hesitated a moment, as if afraid her next words might hurt him. "Neil, I'm practically engaged to Peyt English."

Neil felt a quick lancing pain, and he supposed his eyes must have betrayed him, for Ruth's hand came out, grasping his. She didn't say anything, only stood there looking up unhappily at him.

There was tact in her silence, and Neil was grateful to her. He stayed another ten minutes, talking of this and that, his manner pleasant but guardedly formal. When he left he shook Ruth's hand, and he saw a mild reproof in the blue eyes, as though this were not quite the sort of relationship Ruth had wanted for them.

Women, he thought, as he made his way toward the center of town, never were entirely sure of what they wanted. It had been part of his dream to take Ruth out to Stirrup with him, as the ranch's mistress. He should have known better. Ruth wasn't the sort to sit around waiting patiently for six long years, while a man did his maturing.

Neil took his disappointment into the first saloon he came to when he reached Main Street. It was Bill Ralston's Crescent. He snapped one whisky down quickly, and was pouring himself another when Peyt English came into the place and walked down along the bar to him.

"Got a moment?"

"Sure," Neil said. He nodded down at the bottle. "You a drinking man, English? Help yourself."

English gave a stiff shake of his handsome head. He turned, walking toward a small green-baize-covered table at the rear of the room. Neil followed, taking the bottle and his glass along and placing them on the table between himself and Peyt English.

He sat down then and waited, deliberately patient, while English studied his well-kept smooth hands.

"Your deal, friend," Neil said finally.

English said, "Ruth Orr is a damned nice girl, Ashton."

Neil frowned. "I'll check to that," he said mildly.

"I intend to marry her," Peyt English stated.

Neil regarded the man, feeling a hot envy of English's luck, and trying not to show it. "So she tells me," he said.

"I understand you and Ruth used to be—" English's mouth turned wry, as if he hated to say this—"friendly with each other, Ashton."

It was on the tip of Neil's tongue to say, "Better than that, friend," but he thought better of it. All he said was a quiet "That's right."

English's eyes came up at him across the small table. "I hear Frank Buckmaster has told you to unload that ranch you've inherited and shake dust on this part of the country."

"That's right," Neil said again. He was frowning now, wondering at the direction this talk had taken.

"Under the circumstances," English said, his voice clogging a little with emotion, "it might be better for all concerned if you took Frank's suggestion."

"Wait a minute, my friend," Neil said, pushing his chair back, and he stood up. His legs wedged themselves against the lip of the table, and without thinking what he was doing he let his upper body incline toward English. "Now," he said in an ominously soft voice, "what were you saying?"

English surprised him. "Keep away from Ruth Orr," he blurted. He stood up too, and shoved his chair back. "You're no good. Everybody around here but her seems to know it."

Neil could feel the sudden sharp catching of his breath and the stiffening of his face muscles. There is a limit, he thought, to the price a man should be asked to pay for the past, for his youthful errors of judgment.

One way to invite this sort of thing was to accept it, he knew. He rammed his weight against the table, upsetting his glass and the bottle, and at the same time shoving English back.

The table must have hurt English as it hit his legs, for a wild anger suffused his handsome face. He swore, and dug a hand down inside his black coat.

Neil knew then that the man must be packing a derringer in a shoulder holster. English had apparently gone berserk. He wasn't accountable for his actions, Neil saw.

Neil's own hand dropped to the gun at his hip. He ground

his teeth in frustration, realizing that he could not use lead on Ruth Orr's fiancé, not even to save his own neck.

He swept the table aside, leaping forward, and rammed English back against the wall.

English was still trying to get the shoulder gun out. It had snagged on his coat's lining. Neil hit the man on the upper arm, saw how that blow crippled him, and hit him quickly again, this time on the smooth, well-shaped chin.

Peyt English's stocky body went limp. He slithered down the wall to a sitting position and sat there breathing hard, fingering his welted chin. He looked up at Neil, his pale blue eyes blazing.

The derringer, Neil saw, had come free of the coat lining and had fallen to the floor. Neil bent to pick up the small weapon, unloaded it, and handed it to Peyt English.

"Don't try anything like that again," he said softly. "Next time I may be feeling ringy."

English glared at him, not speaking. Neil eyed him a moment, speculating on the man's temper, then turned down along the bar toward the swing doors. The fat barman, who had witnessed the fight, asked anxiously, "What about that bottle of whisky? Who's going to pay for it?"

Neil hesitated, and then he grinned. He jerked a thumb over his shoulder.

"Him," he said, and he went out then.

Chapter Three

HE TOOK the stage road out of town, veering off it shortly to follow a dug road that carried him slantingly northward through rough stony country.

He put Lodge Creek behind him and pushed up onto the Bench. This remembered tableland was seemingly limitless in extent, and pocked with small swales, none of which held water now.

This range was painfully hard up for water, but in some depressions where last winter's snow had lain late, he saw, the thick tawny grama grass was a foot high. A man could

24

ride a thousand miles and find no better graze. His pride perked up at the thought that he owned a share of this grass now.

An hour's ride brought him in sight of Jules Le Bon's horse ranch, the 66, which lay in a cottonwood grove on a bend of one of Lodge Creek's branches. Neil saw a rider swing out from behind the 66 barn and come out the lane.

It was Lena Le Bon, old Jules's daughter, and he reined in, grinning faintly.

"I had a hunch it was you, Neil," the girl called as she rattled up within earshot. "Mind if I ride along part way to Stirrup?"

The last time he'd seen Lena she'd been a scrawny four-teen-year-old, with a mouth and eyes much too big for the rest of her. Eying her appreciatively now, he thought, Pretty enough to drive a bunkhouse crew crazy, and I reckon she knows it.

"Do you want to?" he asked, lifting his eyebrows.

Lena smiled, her dark eyes touching his, and asked archly, "Do you bite?"

"It seems to be the general idea in Piperock."

Lena puckered her slightly pug nose, reminding him for an instant of the freckled gamin she'd been, the little girl who'd followed him around almost like a dog, on those rare occasions when she had accompanied her father on visits to Stirrup years ago.

"I've heard some of the talk going around, Neil. Frank's certainly done his share of it. People oughtn't to listen. They don't know what you've had to contend with. They don't know what a bitch you had for a stepmother."

"Belle's dead, Lena," Neil pointed out, frowning.

"I don't care. She was a bitch. I'll still say it."

Neil told himself that Lena was only a kid and didn't know any better. They idled along, Lena's little bay pony breaking gait occasionally to keep up with the gray's reaching trot.

"How's your father?" Neil asked. "Is he home?"

"He's never home." Lena's tone was bitter. "He's on his way over to Fort Russell with some horses he hopes to unload on the Army. Why?"

25

"Just wondered," Neil murmured, "what he'd think of your choice of a riding companion."

"Don't be silly, Neil. Dad always liked you." She saw his skeptical grin. "Well, anyway, he never really disliked you. He's always thought of you as a frisky colt that's been badly mishandled. He blames Belle for all that cutting up you did before you left this part of the country."

Neil fell silent, embarrassed. Lena pulled her bay pony close and reached out impulsively, laying her hand on his wrist.

"I've always been strong for you, Neil," she murmured. "I think you must know that."

The huskiness of her voice surprised him, and so did the gesture. It was the gesture of a grown woman, not of the scrawny kid he remembered.

As Lena spoke, a movement of her horse caused her thigh to brush against Neil's leg at the knee, and that brief warm contact sent a little tingle of excitement racing through him. This girl with her huge brown eyes and her hair dark as jet, with her perfectly proportioned small body, had a provocative appeal that no man could ignore, and Neil guessed that Lena was aware of the effect her nearness had on him.

She smiled boldly, invitingly into his eyes. "Stop in and say hello sometime, Neil," she said coquettishly, "on your way to or from town."

The little hussy, Neil thought, but he was smiling tolerantly as he thought it, for it was hard to resent the friendliness Lena had put into her invitation.

"I'll do that, Lena," he murmured, and he pushed on up the road, oddly self-conscious, wondering at the change six years had wrought in Lena and in his own attitude toward her. He could feel her eyes focused on him as she sat her pony in the road behind him, and he supposed she was having her quiet little laugh at him now.

He didn't mind, he decided. Lena was not like the town of Piperock. She took a man as she found him. She didn't judge him, or listen to rumors about him. Neil liked that.

He passed the spring-fed lake half a mile south of Stirrup headquarters and pulled into the yard just at dusk. At first glance he didn't notice anything out of the ordinary about

26

this familiar scatter of buildings. Then he caught the sharp odor of dust on the air, and saw that the turf on the yard had been recently hoof-marked by a large group of horsemen.

The bunkhouse windows, he noticed, had been shot out. Not one whole pane of glass remained. He had an inkling of what to expect now, and he lifted a shout, trying to raise somebody, wondering where his crew might be.

There was no answer. He went over to the bunkhouse and found it a shambles, straw ticking scattered all over the floor, the potbelly stove upended, the crude table at which the men had played their poker games and written their letters knocked to pieces.

There was a note pinned up inside the door, and all it said was: "Don't take too much time making up your mind."

Neil stood there a moment. Frank, he thought angrily, wasn't wasting much time. Neil straightened things up as well as he could in the bunkhouse, and then crossed the yard to the ranch house.

The office was as he remembered it, a tiny cubicle whose walls were decorated with Indian curios and trophies of the hunt. The mangy bearskin rug still tried vainly to cover the floor. The big roll-top desk in the corner still gave the room an illusion of being even smaller than it was.

Neil sat at the desk. Often as a toddler, he remembered, he had come in here and clambered up on his father's knee, and insisted upon being told a story. And he had always been told one, although his father had been hard at work before the distraction.

It came to him that there was something symbolic in this moment. Sitting at this desk, in this very same chair, his father had dreamed his dreams, made his plans for the ranch. My turn now, Neil thought, a lump in his throat, and then he saw the envelope on the desk, with his name printed on it.

It was a note from a man named Bill Marion, his foreman, and it said: "Am writing this in case you come in while me and boys are away and wonder why the place is deserted. Some of your beef has been drifting across the state line into Nebraska. Me and the boys took out after them early this morning. Be back the night after tomorrow."

It was signed without flourish, dated this day. Which meant that if Neil stayed put he would have to wait two days to find out what sort of crew he had inherited from Belle Ashton.

He was in the saddle at dawn, heading east. He made his noon halt across the state line, in Nebraska. The sun was down behind the distant peaks of the Laramie range by the time he located his crew and his drifted cattle.

Topping a rise, he saw the beef, about a hundred head, bedded down for the night on a grassy flat beside a meandering stream.

Four men hunkered over a fire down by the creek bed under some willows. Neil rode toward them. He halted and identified himself a hundred yards out. A husky redhead with a jutting jaw motioned him in. Neil's manner toward this aggressive-looking fellow was designedly pleasant.

"Bill Marion?" he asked, as he stepped down by the fire.

"That's me."

Neil introduced himself. The redhead looked him up and down, something challenging in his eyes, and offhandedly identified his companions. Neil inclined his head toward each man in turn, and then frowned. "That the Stirrup crew nowadays? Four men, counting you?" he asked the redhead.

"There's one other man," Bill Marion said. "The Kid, Jonesy." He saw Neil's puzzled frown, and said almost curtly, "Don't ask me what his front name is. All I know is he ain't bragging about it. He answers to Kid, or plain Jones."

"Where is he?" Neil asked.

"He's got a girl down in Piperock. I figured me and the boys could handle this jag, so I let him run in and see her. He'll probably be waiting for us when we get back to the ranch. Anything wrong in that?"

Neil frowned. There was cockiness in this redhead. The man had undoubtedly conducted Stirrup's affairs pretty much as he pleased, as Belle Ashton's foreman. He would not give up his authority without a struggle, Neil decided as he eyed the fellow.

"Let's take a walk," Neil said.

Bill Marion said, "Sure," and Neil saw the wink he threw at his companions.

They walked upstream, silent until they had put a screen of bushes between themselves and the men at the fire.

"Let's get straight with each other, Bill," Neil said pleasantly. "I need a crew. Right now, as it happens, I'd be in a bad way without one. But I don't put up with insolence from any man working for me. I rod my own outfit."

The redhead grinned at him. Truculence seemed almost to ooze out of the man, but Neil couldn't respond to it with anger. He could understand Marion's reluctance to start taking orders.

"I'd better tell you," Neil said, "Frank Buckmaster has ordered me out of this country. I found the bunkhouse a shambles, and a note of warning from Frank. He's always hated the way I crease my hat. He claims he won't have a man who's been jailed under suspicion of rustling for a ranching neighbor. That's window dressing. I'd give odds he wants to push me out and get hold of the ranch for himself."

"Would you?"

Neil nodded. "He'll be on my tail every minute I stay in this country. He'll be on the trail of any man who works for me."

Marion's grin was cocky, and distracted. Neil knew suddenly that the redhead was trying to work up a fight, looking forward to it with the happy anticipation of a man to whom a fight comes under the heading of recreation.

"There'll probably be some broken heads and some new graves around here before Frank and I settle our differences," Neil warned him. "Are you staying or quitting?" He regarded the man, trying not to appear anxious.

"A fight wouldn't make me quit."

"I've got to know," Neil said mildly.

"Don't rush me," Marion grumbled. "I never saw you before a few minutes ago, friend. I ain't in the habit of judgin' a man on the basis of hearsay, but—" He stopped.

"But what?"

The redhead glanced up, a cool impudence in his gray-green eyes. "Some of the say I been hearing about you ain't pretty."

29

Neil studied the man for a brief moment, then unhooked his gun belt from around his waist and dropped it to the ground. The redhead followed suit, grinning. Their eyes met as they squared off, and Neil, impressed by the confidence in Marion's glance, whipped his fist out, hooking to the man's freckled temple. He was out to finish this quickly, impressively if he could.

Bill Marion went down as if shot, rolled over onto hands and knees, shook his head like a dog, and stood up. He was still grinning. He came running at Neil, swinging one hand.

Neil's head moved to avoid the blow. He poured all his strength into a pile-driver punch to Marion's midsection. It brought a huffing gasp from the man, brought the freckled face down within range of Neil's follow-up punch, a short right to the ear.

Marion went down again, but he came bouncing up like a ball and ran at Neil, punching wildly. Neil hit him hard in the body, not wanting to mark him if he could help it. Marion stepped back, sick but still grinning gamely. He came forward again, and Neil, liking the man now, regretfully crossed his right to the jutting chin.

That was all, and he had to take off his hat and carry water from the creek to revive the redhead. "You asked for it, Bill," he said wearily, watching him sit up and sleeve off his wet face. "I suppose you'll be wanting your time now."

Marion clambered to his feet and used his hat to slap dirt off his Levis. His glance touched Neil's briefly, brittlely, then he turned his back on Neil and returned to the fire.

There wasn't much talk in the little camp by the streamside that night. Neil tried a half-dozen conversational openers, but gave up trying to be sociable after receiving only a series of grunts in reply.

He sat cross-legged and stared into the fire, aloof from Bill Marion and the others, but refusing stubbornly to be frozen out of a camp that was, in the final analysis, his.

They got the beef off bed ground early the next morning. By late afternoon they were idling in toward headquarters, having turned the errant cattle loose on home graze.

As Stirrup buildings poked up over a final rise, Neil saw

30

better than a dozen horses standing ground-hitched in the yard. He and Bill Marion, on speaking terms now, exchanged frowning glances and put spurs to their horses.

Nearing the buildings, Neil saw that the animals in the yard wore the Broken Bit brand. An ingrained sense of caution made him hesitate for an instant. Then he reflected that he owned this outfit now, and he led his four-man contingent of riders boldly into the yard.

Passing a corner of the barn, he saw a tableau that made him pull in on the gray abruptly, that sent a hot sense of outrage coursing through him.

Frank and his Broken Bit riders were lounging idly under the long wagon shed, watching Johnny Winema administer a brutal beating to a fuzzy-faced youngster with apple cheeks, a button nose, and a pair of impudent Irish blue eyes.

Neil knew without asking that this must be the Kid, Jonesy, the member of his crew that he hadn't met yet. The Kid was a tough little game cock, but his arms were too short to let him get in a decent punch at Winema.

His face was a bruised, puffy mess. Blood had matted his straw-yellow hair, and one of his eyebrows was cut to the bone. A flap of skin as big as a half dollar hung down from the cut, forming a grisly eye patch.

The sight of it made Neil's skin crawl. Frank, he noticed, was watching the uneven set-to with callous indifference. Several of the Broken Bit men had turned for a look at Neil and his men as they rounded the corner of the barn, but Frank continued to watch Winema work on the battered youngster. He was too studiously ignoring Neil's presence, and Neil knew then that Frank had known he was riding in, and had staged this brutal tableau especially for him.

That would be like Frank, who was arrogant to the core; and now Neil could feel Bill Marion watching him with a gauging attention, and he mentally tipped his hat to Frank's shrewdness. He was on trial here, he saw. The crew he had inherited from Belle Ashton would judge him by the way he rose to this occasion.

He gigged the gray horse over toward Frank. "Tell Winema to lay off the Kid, Frank."

31

Frank glanced up and nodded. "All right, Johnny," he said.

Winema gave the Kid a last ringing cuff on the cheek that sent him sprawling, and turned away, shrugging.

"See how it goes, do you?" Frank asked. He had his back against the shed post, and he was working on a cigar, as usual. He flicked ash from it. Confidence was in that casual gesture. Frank, after all, had brought a dozen men down here with him. "You damn fool," he said, almost pleasantly, "why don't you chuck in your cards?"

Neil was watching the Kid, who had crawled into the shade of the barn and was lying there like a hurt animal. Winema, Neil saw, wore a simpering smile, a smile that indicated pride in the job he'd done on the youngster.

Neil regarded the copper-skinned man a moment, then unbuckled his gun belt and draped it over the saddle horn. He stepped down off the gray horse and walked over toward Johnny Winema.

The copper-skinned man stared at him, at first surprised and faintly amused, then not so amused. His hand dropped to his gun, and he said, "Don't come no closer."

Neil's stride broke. He regarded the half-breed, and spoke to Frank over his shoulder.

"Tell him to take off the gun, Frank."

He heard Frank's dry laugh behind him. "Why in hell should I?"

"Figure it out for yourself," Neil said. "He may shoot me. If he does, he'll hang for it, and you'll be in some hot water for letting it happen. Unless," he added dryly, "you propose to make a slaughter of this, and not leave any of us alive to tell what happened."

There was a tense silence for a moment. And then Frank was saying, "It looks as if he wants some of what you gave the Kid, Johnny. Why don't you take off the gun and accommodate him?"

Winema frowned, not too happy about the way this had worked out. But there was a lot of vanity in the copper-skinned man. He took off his gun belt and dropped it to the ground. He smiled to show that he wasn't worried.

Neil leaped at him then, knowing the value of the first

punch, and drove his fist into the breed's twisted face. The blow stung Winema. He put his greasy head down and came driving in, butting Neil in the chest. He brought his head up grindingly against Neil's chin.

Neil could smell the man, smell the grease in the unkempt hair. He brought his knee up into the man's stomach, remembering how Winema had worked on him that first day back in Piperock.

He heard Winema let out his breath in a painful grunt. Now, Neil knew, was the time to hit out and seize the initiative. He caught Winema by an arm, swung him like a skater, and sent him crashing against the barn.

Winema bounced off the wood, kicking. Neil grabbed the man's lifted foot, yanked it upward, and upended him. Winema's back was to him briefly as he came erect. He turned, and Neil caught the flash of the knife the fellow had produced from somewhere under his clothing.

It was a stubby knife with a double-edged blade that had been broken off short and sharpened to a new point. It was an ugly, efficient-looking little weapon. There was killing anger in Winema's black eyes as he came at Neil, ready to slash with the knife.

Neil backed away, wariness in him. He was half expecting Frank to order Winema to drop the knife, but Frank didn't speak. Winema ran at Neil, swiping at him with the knife.

Out of the corner of his eye Neil saw the broken segment of a wheel spoke lying on the ground, and he fell toward the short length of wood. His fingers closed around the makeshift bludgeon, and he rolled away as Winema launched a dive at him.

Neil was on his feet first. As the half-breed came erect, Neil struck with the wheel spoke at the hand that held the knife, and hit the man across the knuckles.

Winema snarled out an oath and let the knife fall to the ground. Neil closed with him, catching him by the front of the shirt, lifting him to his toes. He backed the man over against the barn.

He poured it into the man then, left, right, left, wicked blows that punctured the coppery skin. Winema's right hand was no good to him, and he wilted visibly under this treat-

33

ment. When his face was battered into a condition approximating that of the Kid's, Neil stepped back.

Propping himself against the building, Winema wiped blood from his mouth with the back of one hand and stared at Neil with something snakelike in his black eyes.

Neil retrieved his gun belt and strapped it on. Then he picked up Winema's gun belt and knife and handed them to Frank.

"See how it goes, do you, Frank?" he asked.

The big man looked at him without expression. "If I were you," he said, "I wouldn't feel cocky. You were lucky. Next time he'll kill you."

"Next time you and your boys come calling here," Neil said, "You'd better come shooting. Now get out of here, Frank."

"You don't seem to get the idea," Frank said. "You're the one that's getting out, clear out of this country. What do I have to do to convince you I'm not fooling?"

"This is private property, Frank. You and your men are trespassing."

Frank stood there for a silent moment, his eyes hooded, thoughtful. His glanced shuttled over toward where Bill Marion and the rest of Neil's men sat their horses, getting an earful of this conversation. His eyes came back to Neil's, and Neil saw something foxy in them.

"You seem to think I can't run your tail off this range. Maybe you'll tell me what's to prevent it."

"The law, Frank, for one thing."

"Let's see." Frank grinned. "That'd be Roy Millership, down in Piperock. And there's where Roy stays. His badge doesn't mean anything outside of town limits. And then there's the county sheriff. I haven't been to Cheyenne to pay my respects to Tobe Hendy lately, but if I know him, he'll take the view this is strictly between you and me. Another damn range war." He shrugged.

Neil didn't say anything, and Frank asked suddenly, "How many men have you got, friend?" Neil only looked at him, and the big man indicated the Kid and the men grouped around Bill Marion. "We're lookin' at them. I guess there's no need of asking. Six men includin' yourself," he said, and he snorted. "I've got twenty."

Neil frowned. "So?"

"So who wins," Frank said, "if we make it a range war and start trading men off?"

There wasn't any good answer to that, Neil knew. He held to his bitter silence, and Frank siad, "I'd think about it," and then turned to Neil's riders. "And if you boys are at all smart, you'll think about it."

Buckmaster nodded to his men. They sauntered arrogantly across the yard to their horses, and Frank led them out aboard his enormous strawberry roan.

Neil went over to the pump for a cupful of water, which he carried across the yard to the Kid. The youngster was in obvious pain, but he forced a cocky grin as he sipped the water.

He regarded Neil boldly as Bill Marion made the belated introduction.

"Tell us about it, Kid," Neil suggested.

The Kid shrugged scrawny shoulders "Nothin' much to tell. They were waitin' here, an hour ago, when I come in from town. Frank asked me if I'd like a job ridin' for him. I said I'd worked for this iron pretty near a year, and figured to keep workin' for it, at least until I had a look at the new owner. Frank told that damn halfbreed to see what he could do about changin' my mind."

"I see," Neil said. There was a long silence now, while Bill Marion and the others studied the Kid's battered face. They might, Neil knew, remain loyal, threat or no threat, to the iron they had been representing. But what right did he have to accept such loyalty from them? He tried to keep his voice steady as he said, "You can have your time, Kid, whenever you want it."

The Kid was insulted. "Who said anything about quitting?"

Neil grinned his surprise. "Trips to town will have to be out for a while, Kid," he said, "if you stay with the outfit."

The Kid's cut mouth tightened. "I never signed on for no prison sentence," he grumbled. "I've got a girl in town. I told her I'd see her on Sunday."

35

Neil frowned. He was not going to have the Kid run the risk of another beating.

"That's out," Neil said quietly, and his glance flicked around at the others. "The rule applies all the way around, boys, if you're thinking of staying."

There was silence then, while each man debated. The Kid turned to Bill Marion as his champion.

"Bill," he said, "are you going to stand for it?"

Neil could feel the redhead's gray-green eyes swinging on him. "I guess it's a case of quit or take orders, isn't it?" he asked mildly. "He owns the outfit now, Kid."

Neil's relief made him momentarily weak. He shuttled a glance of gratitude at the foreman. Marion acknowledged it with a little jerk of his head. He idled across the yard, indicating that he wanted some private words with Neil now.

Neil spoke to the others. "Take the Kid into the bunkhouse. Paste that eyebrow back in place, so he won't be disfigured."

They nodded. Neil waited until they had taken the Kid into the bunkhouse before walking across the yard to where Marion waited.

"One thing you and me'd better get straight," the redhead said bluntly.

"What's that, Bill?"

"We're going to keep this fight with Frank clean."

Neil frowned. "You saw what just happened. You heard what Frank said. It seems he prefers to fight dirty."

"We'll keep our side of it clean," Marion insisted. Neil stared at the man, wondering at the unrealistic position he'd taken.

"Thought I'd made it clear to you yesterday, Bill, that I give the orders for Stirrup."

"Sure. Sure you give the orders. As long as I approve of the orders. Because where would you dig up another crew for yourself, friend, if I pulled out and took this bunch with me? And don't for a minute think they won't quit if I decide to."

Neil stared puzzledly at the redhead. "What sort of a game are you playing with me, Bill?"

"I never free-rein a horse until I'm sure I can trust it. I

36

feel kind of responsible for that gang in the bunkhouse."

There was no real censure behind the words, and oddly, Neil felt no resentment. He could see Bill Marion's viewpoint. He grinned now, still liking the man. "All right, Bill," he said quietly, and Marion looked at him, a little awkward and ashamed of himself now that he'd put his point over.

He said, "This ruling against anybody riding to town is going to be kind of hard to enforce. I don't know how long you're planning to keep us holed in here, but it happens we're fresh out of salt, and running kind of low on tobacco."

Neil thought a moment. "Make up a list," he said. "I'll ride in for what's needed."

Marion frowned. "Ain't that askin' for trouble?"

"My fight," Neil said, "before it was yours, Bill. Any risks to be run, I'm the one who's going to run them. Make up that list."

The ride to Piperock was without incident. He bought the things Marion seemed to think they'd be needing, and then rode down Main Street to Third Street, where he turned down toward Ruth Orr's place.

Ruth opened the door almost immediately in response to his knock. It was near dusk, and she was dressed to go out, in a simple dress of dark blue that clung to the curves of her figure. Her hair was caught up in a bun at the back, exposing pretty ears. She seemed surprised to see him.

"Won't you come in?" she said warmly. "I'm expecting Peyt English to drop by, but not for a few minutes."

Neil hesitated, then followed her along the narrow hall to the kitchen. It was getting dark out now, and Ruth turned up the wick in the hanging oil lamp, then turned slowly to face Neil.

She had never looked more appetizing, and it gnawed at something inside him to think she'd prettied herself up like this for Peyt English. He shook his head ruefully at her.

"Ruth, I'm just beginning to realize what an idiot I was for ever leaving this part of the country."

Ruth blushed; then that curious gravity came into her eyes. She went over and sat at the table, motioning Neil into the chair across from her. "Neil, don't," she pleaded. "You mustn't say things like that to me."

37

"Why not?" he asked. He nodded down at Ruth's hands, which lay clasped atop the table's oilcloth-covered surface. "I don't see any engagement ring on your finger."

"You will," Ruth said, "before long."

"That my cue to wish you happiness and drop out of the running?" Neil murmured. He shook his head, grinning. "Not till you're wearing his ring, Ruth. A man's not licked till he quits."

Ruth had not seen his grin, and she was nettled. "Are all men so vain?" she asked.

"Don't forget that we knew each other pretty well in the old days," Neil reminded her quietly. "I know what's in you, Ruth. You're not a fickle sort. If you loved me once, there must be a little something left of it."

"Love can be killed, like anything else."

Neil's eyes probed hers. "Do you love this man English?"

"I— You have no right to ask that," Ruth protested.

"Do you?" Neil was still smiling, but Ruth wouldn't look at him.

"I'm going to marry him," she said, and she rose, her glance swinging around at the kitchen clock. "Peyt's due any second. You'll have to excuse me now, Neil."

He followed her out onto the porch, his steps dragging, a deep dissatisfaction in him. Peyt English, he saw, was just turning in through Ruth's front gate.

There was enough daylight remaining to let Neil see the grumpiness on English's face as the man climbed the steps, and he was careful to hide his amusement now as he put out his hand.

"Evening, English," he murmured.

His extended hand touched only air. English looked past his shoulder, pretending not to see the proffered hand. Neil let it fall easily to his side, holding his temper for Ruth's sake.

"Night, Ruth," he said, as though the incident were already forgotten. He walked down the porch steps.

"Neil?" Ruth called, and he swung around, peering back at her. "Be careful on your way back to the ranch."

There was deep concern in her voice. It was her way, Neil supposed, of making amends for English's behavior. But knowing Ruth as he did, he knew that her concern for his safety was genuine. The thought warmed him as he let himself out through the gate.

Ruth watched him climb aboard the gray horse and ride along Third Street toward Main, and then she turned for a cold look at Peyt. It was her instinct, whenever possible, to avoid dissension, but she knew she could not afford to let Peyt's rudeness go unremarked.

"That was pretty pointed, wasn't it, Peyt?" she asked quitely.

"What?"

"You might have shaken hands," Ruth said.

"If it's all the same to you, Ruth, I'd rather not discuss it."

Ruth was puzzled, and vaguely concerned. This wasn't like Peyt. Ordinarily he had perfect manners. That was one of the things that had impressed her about him, six months ago, when he had first come to Piperock. That, and the town's evaluation of him as the handsomest, most eligible bachelor around.

"There shouldn't be anything you and I can't discuss, should there, Peyt?" Ruth asked slowly.

"A man's got to draw the line somewhere," he said, and Ruth found herself frowning.

"What line?"

"I'm a little choosy who I shake hands with," Peyt said. "That fellow's no good, and it happens I know it."

It was the first time she'd heard him adopt such a tone, and Ruth's frown deepened. She had thought she understood Peyt pretty well, but now, listening to him blandly condemn a man he had not laid eyes on until a few days ago, she couldn't help wondering what sort of man Peyt was, really.

Peyt's father, she knew, was some sort of big financial wheel down in Texas. It was his father's money, not Peyt's, that had gone into the ranch out on Sunk Creek.

It is hard to gauge a man to whom things come without effort. And because Ruth knew, with a woman's sure intuition, that her happiness would depend to a large extent

39

upon the character of the man she married, she felt a deepening curiosity about Peyt now.

"Neil and I are old friends, Peyt," she said mildly.

"I'm afraid that doesn't alter my opinion of the fellow."

"That's not very flattering to me," Ruth pointed out dryly.

"Ah—" Peyt reached out suddenly, grasping her by both shoulders. "Haven't we had enough of this?" He used one hand to cock up Ruth's chin, so that she had to meet his demanding eyes.

Ruth looked uncertainly at him. He would have kissed her then if she hadn't twisted out of his arms. He stood frowning at her a moment.

"What's the matter with us, Ruth? What's happening to us?"

"I don't know," she said, and wondered if she were being quite honest. Could Neil have been right when he said she was still a little bit in love with him?

Chapter Four

LENA RODE into Stirrup two weeks later on her little bay pony. Neil went out to the head of the lane to greet her. His crew had come out of the bunkhouse to get an eyeful of the girl. He didn't like that, but he didn't say anything to them about it.

Two weeks' confinement to Stirrup headquarters had given these men a touch of cabin fever, and Neil knew they were on edge, bored and avidly watchful for anything that might offer a break in the routine.

"No time for you to be this far from Sixty-six, Lena," he said as she reined up before him. He inclined his head toward the lowering sun. "Be dark before you get home."

"Then you'll just have to escort me, won't you?" Lena smiled.

Neil looked at her without expression for a moment, then sighed, calling over his shoulder, "Kid, catch up my gray, will you?"

The Kid nodded, somewhat sullenly, Neil thought, and went over to snake Neil's animal out of the corral. Meanwhile, Lena was flashing her brilliant smile at the rest of Neil's crew.

They touched the brims of their hats with meager politeness. All except Bill Marion, who deliberately ignored the girl's presence. Neil wondered about that, but promptly forgot all about it as the Kid brought him his horse.

"Enjoy yourself," the Kid said, as he gave Neil the reins. He sounded sore about something.

"Not exactly a pleasure jaunt, Kid," Neil said dryly.

"Neil, I think I resent that." Lena laughed. Neil noticed that the Kid couldn't keep his eyes off her. Lena had a delicately ripening beauty that fairly cried out to be looked at, and the Kid was human.

Neil rose to the saddle and gigged the gray out the lane, pulling Lena's bay along with him.

"You shouldn't have come here, Lena," he told her.

"Well, really!"

Neil told her about the beating the Kid had received from Johnny Winema, and about the Kid's girl in Piperock.

"I can't hold him prisoner here on Stirrup forever," he said. "The kid's at the girl-crazy age, Lena. He'll climb the fence sooner or later." Neil sighed, thinking of the others. "They're all pretty sick of hanging around headquarters trying to think of jobs to keep them busy. But I haven't much choice of tactics. I'm playing the waiting game with Frank, using time for a weapon."

Lena bit at a ripe lower lip and was silent. They topped a rise and idled downgrade toward Stirrup's spring lake, with its scrubby willow border.

Neil's horse nickered plaintively. Neil let the animal carry him down off the road toward the water.

Lena's bay followed. At the water's edge she dropped to the ground, and pointed at a patch of green grass under one of the willows. "Let's sit a minute."

They sat watching a brown bug skitter across the water. Above, in a tree, a swamp sparrow scolded. It was cool here, and pleasant. Neil nibbled a grass tip in idle contentment.

41

"The waiting game," Lena said, "isn't like you, Neil. Not the you I remember."

Neil's slow shrug was bitter. Ordinarily he would never have given the initiative to Frank. It was Neil's instinct, when hit, to counterpunch at once, with a vengeance. He was crippled by concern for the safety of his men, who owed him nothing. And he felt at a disadvantage in this fight because of his reputation.

The rumors Frank had spread about him were certain to hurt him in Piperock, where he was remembered as a young hellcat. He must walk softly now, Neil knew; otherwise he would be playing into Frank's hands.

And there was the problem of his redheaded foreman. He told Lena how matters stood just now between him and Bill Marion.

"Well, the nerve!" Lena said. "In other words, Bill Marion is telling you what to do." Neil failed to notice the sulky expression that briefly destroyed the symmetry of her small features. "Did you notice how he snubbed me back there?"

"I wondered about that," Neil admitted.

"He doesn't like me," Lena said. "He's never bothered to hide it." Vindictiveness glinted in the black eyes, but her voice was quiet, reasonable as she said, "Fire him, why don't you, Neil? You don't have to take orders from your own foreman."

Neil shook his head, frowning at the suggestion. Lena met his glance, her eyes guileless, and Neil decided this was not spitefulness in her. She glanced down, tracing out a pleat in her black riding skirt.

"Didn't you make any friends for yourself up north, Neil?"

He grimaced. "None I'd care to be seen with in Piperock. My friends up north, until the past year, were mostly beyond the pale. Outlaws. Part-time grifters. Gunmen."

Lena glanced at him. "But that's perfect. That's what Frank's asking for, isn't it? Write them, Neil. Get them down here. Offer them fighting pay, if you have to."

Her earnestness made him smile. Her words had a strange sound, coming out of a pretty young girl's mouth. But it certainly was one way to hit back at Frank, Neil had to admit, and he wondered why it had not occurred to him.

Frank's man Winema was obviously a gunhand, and there was always a case to be made for fighting fire with fire. What was it Frank had said: "Who wins if we make it a range war and start trading men off?"

Neil thought of his crewmen, who had just happened to be on hand when the hard feelings between him and Frank had erupted, and were too proud to quit under fire. They'd all have a better chance of survival if a few professional fighting men were added to the roster at Stirrup.

"I wonder," Neil murmured, "if Bill Marion would stand for it."

"He'd have to," Lena said simply, and Neil, after mulling it over, supposed she was right.

"I know a man up in Sheridan," he mused, "who's fond of money and doesn't care much how he gets it. Bat Gardner. He's a tough little monkey. And he has some hard friends."

"Neil," Lena said, "it's the way." There was something in her expression hard to define. She was like a little girl, keyed up at the prospect of some excitement. Neil frowned at her, and then told himself he was too critical of this pretty girl, who was trying only to be helpful.

"Suppose I write this Bat Gardner a letter, when we get to your place. Could you arrange to have it mailed for me, Lena?"

"I'm driving into Piperock first thing in the morning, as it happens."

Two hours later, after having penned his brief message to Bat Gardner and left it with Lena, Neil was riding out 66's lane through the dark of early evening, wondering if he had done a wise thing.

He heard horsemen approaching, and he slowed as a pair of shadowy figures came along the lane toward him. Neil recognized old Jules Le Bon, Lena's father, and tall, silver-haried John Llewellyn, one of the pioneer ranchers, along with Neil's dad, up here on Bench grass.

"Gentlemen," Neil said. He had not seen either of these men in six years, and his manner toward them now was pleasant, respectful. He knew that in their book he was a

43

horse to be carefully watched, on the basis of past performance.

He was pleased at the friendly warmth with which both of these older men pumped his hand.

"Son, you're looking fine," John Llewellyn said, squinting at him in the deepening dusk. "More and more like your father."

"I'll accept that for a compliment, John," Neil told the silver-haired rancher.

Lena's father wanted to know what had brought Neil down here from Stirrup. Neil told him, and the gray little man with the canny horse trader's eyes thanked him for seeing Lena home safely. If he disapproved of the girl's riding to Stirrup, he did a good job of hiding that feeling.

The talk turned to the prices of horses and cattle, and to the condition of the range.

"This dry weather keeps up," John Llewellyn said, "we'll all be leanin' on that lake water of yours, son."

Neil liked the casualness with which the older man broached the subject. It indicated that John Llewellyn had confidence in him. He said, "The water's there when the need arises for it, John. Pass the word along."

John Llewellyn, as the oldest active cattleman on the Bench, was the delegate for his ranching neighbors in most matters. "I'll do that," the older man said. He shook Neil's hand warmly once more, and then swung along the lane toward the 66 buildings, accompanied by Lena's father.

Neil got back to Stirrup headquarters about nine o'clock. He had led the gray horse into the larger of the two corrals, and was off-saddling when Bill Marion sauntered across from the bunkhouse.

Neil took a deep breath, and then told the redhead about the letter he'd written and left with Lena for mailing. It was a long time before Bill Marion spoke, and then all he said was: "I hope you know what you're doing. I won't pretend that I like the idea, but it's your party. I reckon it's up to you how you run it."

Neil sensed that there was something else on the redhead's mind, something troubling the man, which might account for the mildness of his reaction to Neil's news.

44

"I've got something to tell you," Marion said after a moment. "You won't like to hear this. The Kid's rode to Piperock to see his girl."

Neil swore. "He had orders to stay put here. Why in Sam Hill did you let him go?"

"I argued myself blue in the face,' Marion said, "tryin' to stop him."

"You might have used force on him," Neil said.

"If I had," Marion said, "you'd have one less man workin' for you now. The Kid ain't like me, Neil. You can't use your hands on him. Not and keep him around."

Neil frowned. "I'd better ride in there and see that nothing happens to him."

"Why don't you let it ride?" suggested the foreman. "You run in there now playin' the mother hen, and he'll quit you like a shot. He's a cocky little son. I know how his mind works."

Neil stood there frowning, debating. Marion said, "He swore to me, up and down, that he can skin into town and out again with no one the wiser. He can be pretty tricky when he wants to be. It's his hide. Let him risk it if he wants to, why don't you?"

"Will he come back in one piece?" Neil asked.

"I'm gambling on it," Marion said with conviction.

"I hope you're right," Neil said, and he shook his head, not so convinced of it as he would have liked to be.

Chapter Five

THE BATTERED old clock on the wall ticked off the seconds. Peyt English teetered his chair back, relaxing now as he watched Ruth bustle about making coffee.

He wondered if the fact that he had been asked into Ruth's kitchen tonight, at the unconventional hour of midnight, indicated a change in her attitude toward him.

For two weeks Ruth had held him gently at bay. He blamed Neil Ashton for it. Ruth's, after all, was a friendly, outgoing disposition, Ashton was currently in some trouble, and Ruth could be loyal to a fault sometimes.

She was a bit too loyal toward Ashton, and it was time, Peyt thought, to jog her out of it. His hand strayed into his coat pocket, touching the tiny satin-lined jewel box he had been carrying with him for the better part of a week now and had not yet dared show Ruth.

He rose to hold a chair for her as she came across the room and poured the coffee, and afterward, when they were both seated, he pushed the jewel box across the oilclothed tabletop with the tips of his fingers.

Ruth had set the coffeepot down on a pad. She looked at the jewel box, frowning a little, and then she looked up questioningly into Peyt's eyes.

"Have a look, Ruth," Peyt suggested.

It seemed to him there was something reluctant in the way Ruth picked up the box. She was still frowning as she released the tiny clasp. The lid sprang up. Her eyes went wide and she drew a quick breath, then sat there staring down at the engagement ring Peyt had bought her.

"It's beautiful," she said after a moment. "I—I never knew a diamond could be so beautiful, Peyt."

"Will you wear it?" Peyt asked, watching her, his tension obvious.

"Peyt, I—I'm flattered. I'm really terribly flattered. But—"

"Wait," Peyt said quickly. "Before you say yes or no, let me say something, Ruth. I'm not an impatient man. I think you know that. It could be next year, if you wanted it to be. Right now all I want is my ring on your finger."

Ruth looked up curiously at him. "Why?" she asked gently.

"I guess it's that old devil pride, Ruth." Peyt grinned. "I want people to know."

Ruth shook her head chidingly at him. She was smiling as she snapped the lid of the case down. But then her eyes sobered. "Peyt, the last thing I'd want is to hurt you, but I—I'm not sure."

"You used to be," Peyt said. He saw the heavy rise of her bosom under the bodice of her light dress. A swift sympathy

46

for him came into her eyes, and she reached across the table, covering his hand with her own.

"Don't we owe it to ourselves to be absolutely sure, before we commit ourselves to anything, Peyt?" she asked gravely.

Peyt felt an angry lump in his throat, and he pulled his hand out from beneath Ruth's and returned the ring to his coat pocket. He was behaving childishly, he realized, and he despised himself for it. But it was impossible for him to smile and talk pleasantly now, and put a good face on his disappointment.

He finished his coffee hurriedly and excused himself, afraid that if he stayed too long, he might do or say something foolish.

He took out his disappointment on his white-stockinged sorrel, spurring the animal into a wild run on the way out of town. As he swung off the stage road he cursed the impulse that had betrayed him into proposing tonight. Timing, in affairs of the heart, was an important factor, and—

The flat, thwacking report of a pistol pulled him back with a start against the high cantle of his Mueller saddle. The gun had gone off at some distance. Peyt reined in, squinting northward into the stony country from which the sound had come.

Puzzled, and instantly cautious, he turned his sorrel down off the road onto a carpet of thick grass. He ran along silently, parallel with the road, until he came to the foot of a low dome-shaped hill.

Peyt tied his sorrel in a clump of shadbush and picked his way cautiously up the slope. At the top of the hill he pushed his hat back off his head, letting the neck thong support it against his shoulders, and peered out from behind a boulder imbedded there at the hill's crest.

What he saw made him draw a quick breath and swallow slowly. Below him on a twist of the road two men on horse-back confronted each other. Strong moonlight played on them. Peyt had no trouble recognizing them as Frank Buck-master's hired gunman, Johnny Winema, and that cheeky Kid from out on Stirrup.

Winema, Peyt saw, held a gun in his hand, and the Kid was staring bitterly at the weapon, with his hands lifted.

47

Winema must have laid an ambush for the Kid there, Peyt realized. The shot he had heard had probably been Winema scare-shooting, to teach the Kid the folly of running.

Peyt could hear Winema's voice down below there. "You ain't very bright, are you, Kid?"

"Why?" The Kid sounded sullen, defiant.

"Anybody else would've learned somethin' from that beating I gave you at Stirrup. I'm going to give you some more of the same, Kid. And this time I'm not going to fool around with you. You was warned. You didn't listen."

Winema's voice was cold, impersonal, the voice of a man who laughed at pity. Peyt had heard about that trouble out at Stirrup, about the thrashing Winema had received from Neil Ashton. A thing like that wouldn't sit well with a man like Winema. There wasn't much, Peyt thought anxiously, that the man would stop at by way of retaliation.

He probably ought to take a hand in this. The Kid might even be killed if he didn't. But he gave a sullen shake of his head. It was none of his affair. He would not interfere in it.

He heard Winema say, "Keep those hands nice and high, Kid." He watched, fascinated, as Winema stepped his horse along the road toward the Kid, and then pulled the animal around at the Kid's right and a trifle behind him.

"What is this?" the Kid muttered.

Peyt had a hunch the Kid knew Winema was preparing to relieve him of his gun. It seemed to him the Kid was debating, wondering whether he ought to make a try for the weapon before Winema could tease it out of the holster.

Don't try it, Peyt thought, swallowing slowly. Don't try it.

The Kid peered back at Winema over one scrawny shoulder. His glance appeared to be narrowing down on the back of Winema's right hand, and now Peyt saw the half-breed give a negative shake of his head.

"Two weeks since Ashton hit me in the hand with that wheel spoke, Kid, if that's what you're thinking. I heal pretty quick. So don't get your hopes up, and don't try nothing foolish."

48

The Kid sat there, looking a little crestfallen. The gun in Winema's hand steadied.

"Turn your head and look up the road. Front and center."

The Kid turned his head, his thin shoulders slumping. From where he lay at the crest of the low hill, Peyt heard the creak of Winema's saddle leather. The gunman was leaning out to take the Kid's gun, putting weight on the near stirrup.

It was as though the gunman's gesture, or the creak of the saddle, infuriated the Kid. He was, Peyt knew, a runty youngster who had to be forever asserting his toughness. Apparently the boy had made up his mind he'd be damned if he'd sit his horse like a gutless pup while his gun was taken.

He gave the horse, a sway-backed brindle gelding, knee pressure. The animal jiggled off to one side. Winema, reaching out for the Kid's gun, was thrown off balance by the unexpected maneuver.

The Kid saw that, and he proved his immaturity now by raking the brindle savagely with both spurs. He bent down, Indian style, along the animal's neck, and clawed at his gun as his horse surged forward.

For a moment Peyt almost dared to hope the Kid would make it. Then he heard Winema's foul curse, and he saw the man's hand move, bringing the drawn gun into line with the target.

The Kid was still trying to drag his gun out when Winema's gun bucked and spat at him.

That first shot of the half-breed's straightened the Kid in the saddle. For an agonized instant he held his seat on the running horse, making a picture target for Winema.

Winema's gun spat fire again, and Peyt felt a fluttery sickness at the pit of his stomach as he watched the Kid's body crumple and pitch from the saddle.

Peyt lay in a sort of paralysis, unable to move, almost unable to breathe, his dazed eyes clinging to Winema. The half-breed had reholstered his smoking gun, and he rode over alongside of the Kid's riderless horse now.

Peyt heard the killer speak to the Kid's horse in a soothing tone. He frowned, watching the gunman transfer himself, without touching a foot to the ground, from his own horse to the back of the Kid's horse.

Winema snaked out the Kid's rope, leaned down to slip a loop onto one of the Kid's booted legs, and then spurred the horse, dragging the Kid to the center of a weed-clogged swale fifty yards off the road. He off-dallied, flinging the rope to the ground.

Peyt watched him ride back to where his own horse stood patiently waiting. He got back on his own horse, again without touching the ground, glanced once, briefly, toward the place where he had dragged the Kid's body, and then rattled off up the road, leaving the Kid's horse to its own devices.

And still Peyt lay on top of the hill not moving. He had just witnessed a cold-blooded killing, and he knew what he ought to do now. Contact Cheyenne. Report this to the sheriff's office.

But in doing so he would be handing Neil Ashton victory over Frank Buckmaster, paving the way for Ashton to remain and grow strong in this part of the country. For he knew that if he ever told a jury what he had just seen, Winema would be in very hot water, and Frank would need a smart lawyer to save him from involvement in this.

It was ironical, he thought, that he, of all people, should have been chosen to save the day for Neil Ashton. The thought made him angry, for he was convinced that Ruth would be better off with Ashton out of this country. He fingered the tiny jewel box in his pocket, and, remembering how his proposal to Ruth had been rejected, he knew suddenly that he was going to forget what he had seen.

He picked his way down the slope to his sorrel. As he rose to the saddle and wheeled the animal toward his Sunk Creek headquarters, he tried to shake off the uneasy conviction that there was something wrong, terribly wrong, in what he was doing.

It seemed to Frank Buckmaster that he had been in bed only a few minutes when a rattle of hoofs outside his window brought him back to awareness.

Frank rolled heavily out of the bed, which had a hair

mattress so hard you could bounce a ball on it, and padded across the uncarpeted floor of this Spartan room to the window.

It was Johnny Winema, Frank saw. He pulled his massive, hairy legs into his Levis and barefooted it along the dark hall to the front door. He opened the door and saw Winema standing just outside, a sepulchral figure pale in the moonlight.

"Come in," Frank grunted, and he led the way into the living room, where he lit the Argand lamp on the table. He flung his burned match into the beehive fireplace. "All right," he said curtly, "what's happened?"

Winema glanced shiftily at him. "I been keepin' an eye on the Kid's girl's house, like you told me to, Frank," he mumbled, and he lapsed into an uncomfortable silence.

"The Kid finally paid her a visit, is that it?" Frank asked.

"That's right," Winema said slowly.

Frank's grin was triumphant. "I knew he couldn't stay away from her much longer. The Kid's just found out girls are made different." Winema's eyes, Frank noticed, had dropped to the floor. "What's eating you, Johnny? Stop beating around the bush."

Winema, without glancing up, gave a meager shake of his head.

Frank said, "I told you to waylay the Kid and give him a beating that'd make that other one look like a picnic. Don't tell me you let him skin past you."

"That ain't it, Frank," Winema said. There was something almost sick in his voice, and Frank felt a gray premonition.

"You killed him, didn't you, Johnny?" he asked after a long moment of silence.

"He tried to run for it, Frank. He was draggin' iron when I blew him over. I hadn't no choice but to let him have it. I—"

"You fool!" Frank raged, and his hand whipped out, slapping Winema. The force of Frank's blow and the unexpectedness of it sent the gunman careening backward across the room. He slammed up against the mantel, dislodging from its wooden wall pegs an old Kentucky rifle

51

that had been handed down in Frank's family through three generations, and was Frank's proudest possession.

The ancient, long-barreled weapon struck the stone of the hearth on its butt end, and at an awkward angle. There was a snapping sound, like the exploson of a firecracker, as the dried wood of the hand-carved stock split lengthwise.

For one stricken, horrified instant Frank stared at the priceless old flintlock, and then a wild fury gripped him. He clenched his fists, breathing with difficulty now, and started across the room toward Winema.

A glimmer of animal fear brightened Winema's eyes, and his bronzed hand hovered dangerously over his gun. It was enough to make Frank think twice, for he knew that Winema was fast, that his highly specialized skill with the six-gun was the focus of the man's life. And Frank knew Winema's temper. Frank pulled in a slow breath, eying the half-breed.

"Where is he?" he murmured after a moment, and Winema stared blankly at him.

"Where's who, Frank?"

"The Kid," Frank said. "Where'd you leave him?"

Winema described his effort to conceal the body. He seemed pretty smug as he said, "Nobody's going to tie me to that killing, Frank. My horse never left the road, and I never set foot to the ground."

"What about the Kid's horse?" Frank asked.

"I left him there," Winema said. "Why?"

Frank gave the man a look of disgust. "That horse will probably head straight home to Stirrup. What's left of Neil's crew will be combing the countryside for the Kid in a matter of hours. Neil Ashton can read sign like an Injun. You better hope he doesn't locate the corpse before there's been some morning traffic moving along that road, Johnny."

Winema shifted uneasily from one long leg to the other. "Maybe I better make myself scarce, Frank, till we see how this thing's going to work out."

Frank shook off the suggestion. "If you run now," he growled, "you'll be as good as writing out a confession."

"But—"

"This range," Frank stated flatly, "would hold me respon-

52

sible with you. I'm not having any of that. You'll stick.
We'll brazen this out."

"Suppose we don't get away with it?" Winema asked
bleakly.

"We better," Frank said, and he regarded Winema with
a dark speculation. "Just one thing, Johnny," he said. "Don't
get any ideas between now and morning. I've got some hard
men out there in my bunkhouse." Frank grinned now. "You
wouldn't get far, if you tried to run out."

Chapter Six

IT WAS MID-AFTERNOON when Neil Ashton rode into
Frank Buckmaster's Broken Bit headquarters with the
county sheriff, Tobe Hendy.

Neil had sent for Hendy some hours after sunrise, after
he and Bill Marion had located the Kid's bullet-pierced
body in the jungle growth of a swale north of Piperock.

Neil had been almost constantly with the sheriff since
that heavy-set lawman had stepped off the train in Piperock,
and he still hadn't made up his mind about the man.

"That's Frank's place?" Tobe Hendy asked, lifting a pon-
derous arm to point toward Frank's buildings. Neil nodded,
and Hendy grunted, "You sure he'll be in?"

"He's not in town," Neil said, shrugging. "That's all I
can say for sure, Sheriff."

Tobe Hendy sucked air through his teeth, slumping along
at Neil's side with a fat man's peculiar grace. They hadn't
accomplished much so far, Neil thought, shuttling a glance
at the sheriff. It had rained briefly during the night, oblit-
erating sign around the Kid's body, so they'd been out of
luck there.

Tobe Hendy had interviewed the Kid's girl, had estab-
lished the fact that the Kid had left the girl around midnight. That was about all they had. That, and the fact that
two weeks ago Frank's hired muscle, Winema, had worked
the Kid over.

As they crossed the plank bridge and approached the

Broken Bit buildings, Frank emerged from the house, followed by Johnny Winema. Both men wore puzzled, blandly innocent expressions, and Neil felt anger strike through him. There wasn't much doubt in his mind that one or the other of these men was responsible for the Kid's death. He didn't realize he was grinding his teeth until Tobe Hendy clucked a warning at him.

"Let's not jump to conclusions, Ashton." The sheriff's small eyes, immersed in folds of soft flesh, touched Neil's. "I'll handle this," he said.

Neil's faint nod was reluctant. He trotted on into Broken Bit's yard with the sheriff.

There had been no attempt made to dress up this scatter of ranch buildings. The barns and corrals had a sturdy, workmanlike appearance, but their uncompromising functionalism deprived them of any beauty. This place was a true reflection of the personality of the man who swung the big whip here, Neil decided. All business, and to hell with the side issues.

Frank was standing at the edge of the patio with his big arms akimbo, watching Neil and the sheriff ride in. Winema stood at Frank's side, a respectful pace behind him.

"Hello, Tobe." Frank grinned up easily at the sheriff.

Tobe Hendy frowned at the familiarity of Frank's greeting. There was stiffness in his answering nod. He climbed down off his horse without waiting for an invitation to do so.

Frank's eyes narrowed. His glance touched Neil's briefly, and then he was grinning again, and pivoting to face the sheriff. "How's Cheyenne?"

"Frank," Hendy said, wheezing his words out, "I hear you and Ashton have been jumping the chain at each other."

Frank nodded, and blandly outlined his objections to Neil as a ranching neighbor. Neil's hands clenched at his sides when Frank spoke of his having been jailed for rustling up north, but Hendy threw him a warning glance, and his temper subsided. Viewing this thing objectively, he was forced to admire Frank's strategy. By blandly admitting what was common knowledge, Frank would keep the sheriff guessing.

Tobe Hendy said, "Ashton tells me you had one of his men beaten up, Frank."

54

"That's right." Frank nodded. "The Kid. I offered him a job riding for me, and he got lippy with me. What about it?"

The sheriff's eyes rose speculatively at Frank. "The Kid's horse moseyed into Stirrup in the wee hours of this mornin', Ashton tells me. Blood on the saddle. It took Ashton and his crew three hours to locate the corpus delicti. The Kid had been dragged into some weeds a mile or so this side of town."

Neil was watching Frank, who had let his jaw sag as the sheriff talked. Frank gave Tobe Hendy a straight frowning look, and he was an actor, Neil thought. Frank was not overplaying his role now.

The sheriff said, "You didn't know, Frank?"

"No."

"Where were you last night? Say about midnight?"

"Here," Frank said. "When my crew gets in they'll vouch for it."

"Ask him where Winema was, Sheriff," Neil broke in impatiently. He saw that the sheriff didn't appreciate that interference, but he felt he'd had to say it. There was something maddeningly deliberate about the way the sheriff asked his questions.

"Well, Frank?" Hendy said, and Frank hesitated.

Neil was grinning at Frank now. "Why not let Winema speak for himself, Frank?"

Frank lifted pained eyes at the sheriff, but Hendy's interest had already focused on Johnny Winema.

"Where were you at midnight last night, friend?" he asked, and Neil saw the murderous glance the half-breed flicked at him.

"Here," Winema said.

"And before that?" Hendy presisted.

"Town."

"And you left town when?"

"Nine, nine-thirty," Winema said, shrugging.

"And you came straight nere?"

"That's right," Winema said, and Neil studied Winema's expressionless face, thinking, Like hell you did, Johnny. You rode out of town and waited for the Kid.

"Pass anyone on the way up here, Winema?" the sheriff

asked idly. The copper-skinned man shook his head, and the fat man's rosebud lips pursed. "Odd," he mused. "Seems like *some*body'd be usin' the road, that time of evenin'. We can check on that point, my friend. I hope you realize it."

Neil held his breath, feeling the heavy beat of his heart. The sheriff had baited an old, old trap for a killer. Neil watched Winema.

The half-breed's eyes took on a panicky look, but just for an instant. He shrugged and said idly, "I never followed the road."

"Maybe," Tobe Hendy said caustically, "you'll tell me how come."

Winema glanced toward Frank, whose rigid face did not relax a muscle. The half-breed returned his glance to the sheriff, murmuring, "I always beat my way back here to the ranch across country, if there's any kind of a moon up."

Hendy frowned, no longer sure of his ground, and Neil knew bitterly that he was going to have to take a hand in this, whether the sheriff liked it or not.

"Winema," he said, his eyes probing the half-breed's, "you're a damn liar."

It seemed to him that the man bounced at him then. Winema swung out wickedly at him with a fisted hand. There was the wildness of a hunted thing in the half-breed's black, shining eyes.

Neil was hardly prepared for such a pell-mell attack. He took Winema's knuckles on the mouth. He went staggering back, but did not lose his footing.

He shook his head, wiping a trickle of blood off his lips, and contemplated the half-breed. Two weeks ago he had whipped this man soundly. Apparently the lesson had been wasted, for here he was asking for more of the same, spoiling for trouble.

Neil walked toward Winema, lifting his hands, falling into a fighter's crouch. He was grinning.

"I'm glad you did that, friend," he said.

Winema used the back of his hand to push hair out of his eyes. He was watching Neil, on his guard now.

Tobe Hendy said, "Back off. Both of you. Lower your hackles."

Neil turned his head slightly, and saw that the sheriff had drawn his gun. Neil lifted a pointing hand toward the half-breed. "That's the man that killed the Kid, Sheriff. Give me a minute or two and I'll choke it out of him."

He heard the gun click warningly as Tobe Hendy eared back its hammer.

"I said back off, son," Hendy said. "That's not the way I gather evidence."

Neil glanced at the gun, and then glanced at Winema. Winema was smiling tauntingly at him, and Neil remembered that he had a personal score to settle with this fellow. He took a step forward.

"I wouldn't shoot to kill," Tobe Hendy said, "but I'll sure as hell cut side meat off you, Ashton, if you don't pull your horns in."

Neil pointed a trembling finger at Winema. "That's the man."

"Large statement," said the sheriff. "Can you prove it?"

"No."

"Then if I was you, I'd keep quiet about it."

Winema and Frank exchanged furtive, smug glances at that, Neil noticed. He looked bitterly at the sheriff.

Tobe Hendy saw how he felt, and said, "Have you any idea how big Laramie County is, Ashton? Bigger'n the state of Massachusetts. That's how much territory I've got to keep an eye on. Show me some real evidence against this man—" he nodded at Winema—"and I'll give you some action."

Neil started to speak, but the sheriff silenced him by up-palming one pudgy hand.

"Until then," he suggested, "considerin' your reputation, I'd whistle kind of soft around any man wearin' a law badge if I was you, Ashton."

Frank was grinning openly now, and Neil felt a sour frustration. He had come up against the barrier of his background. He had earned this rebuff, he realized, and he could not find it within himself to resent the position the sheriff had taken.

The fat man had done his duty here, as he saw it. Neil shrugged in defeat, turning his back on the man, and went over to where the gray horse stood ground-reined.

Chapter Seven

ON HIS WAY up 66's lane, Neil Ashton encountered Lena Le Bon on her way out in a light topless carriage. He pulled the gray off the high ground between the wheel ruts and gigged the animal down into the gutter, making room for the carriage.

"Neil," Lena said, reining in to look at him, "I've heard what happened at Frank's place two weeks ago."

Neil looked at her in surprise. He had done no talking about that.

"Frank's such an arrogant fool," Lena explained, "that he's been bragging about it. I think it's an outrage, Neil. Tobe Hendy ought to be thrown out of office."

"Tobe's all right," Neil said, and Lena's pretty mouth went slack.

"Any news?" she asked after a moment, and Neil nodded, guessing what she meant.

"They'll be coming in today or tomorrow," he said "Depending on their luck with train connections."

"Train?" Lena said.

"I wrote again after we buried the Kid," Neil said, "and told them I wanted them down here in a hurry. Is your dad in, Lena?"

"Yes. Why?"

"I'm in the market for four saddle horses."

"Four?" Lena said. "Only four?" She looked disappointed. Neil wondered if it had occurred to her that gunmen cost money.

"You haven't seen these four," he reassured her. "One wolf is worth—let's see—how many dogs?"

Lena shook her pretty head at him. "Neil, I've been thinking it over, and it's no good. Why don't you give them

58

something for their trouble, when they get in, and send them back where they came from?"

He grinned indulgently at her, wondering if all startlingly beautiful girls felt it was their prerogative to be impulsive, and as changeable as the wind.

Lena reddened a little under his gaze, which surprised him.

She said, "There's no chance for you to hold out against Frank up there on Stirrup, Neil. Even after you've taken on these four new men, Frank will still have you outnumbered. He'll make a checker game of it, killing you off one by one, if you don't knuckle down to him."

"Will he?" Neil asked, but a voice inside warned him that Lena was talking sense. The conviction had strengthened in him, since the Kid's death, that Frank wanted Stirrup, and he had a hunch that Frank's ambition would not let him stop once he acquired Stirrup grass and the lake water. Frank's arrogance fed on power to dominate.

Somebody, Neil thought, has got to stop the fellow, and I guess I'm elected.

"There's a way out for you, you know," Lena said.

"Oh?" He glanced curiously at her.

"You could sell Stirrup. If you'd sell out now, I think I could get Dad to take you on at our place." She was watching him closely. "As a partner," she added.

"A partner?" Neil said, his eyes widening.

"Don't look so stunned," Lena said. "Dad's always liked you. Really, I mean it. And I'll let you in on a little secret. Dad's been wanting to expand and go after more Army business. There's a fortune to be made in selling remounts to the Army, Neil, but Dad hasn't been able to promote the cash he needs to go after that business in a big way. If you'd sell Stirrup, you'd have some money available for investment, and—"

"Whoa down a minute," Neil said. His head was spinning.

"Another thing," Lena said. "Dad's too old to be traipsing all over the state to horse auctions. You must know horses if you ran a horse lot up north. You could take over some of Dad's buying. You'd be a godsend to him right now, Neil."

Neil shook his head at her, and Lena said, "What's the matter?"

The matter? Neil thought, and he stared at this piquantly pretty dark-eyed girl, wondering if she could make good on what she so carelessly offered. Lena probably could, he decided. Many times, before he quit Stirrup and this part of the country, he had seen the girl twist old Jules to her will.

Jules doted on her. She was his only child. She was all the old fellow had, really, and he naturally wanted her to be happy. If she convinced him that her happiness depended on this . . . Neil frowned, and left the thought dangling, unfinished. Lena was offering him more, much more, than a partnership in her father's horse ranch, he realized.

She was offering him herself, in effect. He felt a swift hot shame, and a thrust of anger that he did not let Lena see. Nor could he stay angry with her. Warmth and impulsiveness were part of her feminine nature. She was only trying to help, and being young, with the thoughtlessness of a young girl, she had not considered the possible injury to his pride.

"Thanks. I guess not," he said gently. He saw Lena's tiny foot press at the carriage's flooring, saw the rise of color to her pretty cheeks, and so he was prepared, to some extent, for her outburst.

"You fool! You fool!" She slapped the team with her reins and went careening along the rutted lane in the carriage.

Neil looked after her, still indulgently grinning. She'd hate him for a while, he reflected.

It came to him that a woman's hate, when the woman in question was a little spitfire like Lena, could be a dangerous thing, and his grin faltered.

Chapter Eight

FROM HIS BUGGY'S SEAT, where he waited, Peyt English had a partial view of the interior of Adam Bergendahl's store. Ruth, Peyt saw, was still at the counter, consulting her list of groceries to buy, while the old man scooped coffee into a brown paper bag for her.

As always on these Saturday mornings, Ruth was making slow progress with her marketing. Peyt settled back against the seat cushion, prepared to be patient.

In front of Bergendahl's display window, which was empty except for a sprinkling of dead flies and a film of dust from the dry street, four men stood idly conversing. They were a rough-looking lot, strangers to Piperock. They regarded Peyt with the lazy impudence of men having nothing better to do, and after a while it began to get on Peyt's nerves.

Peyt's nerves were none too steady to begin with. For a couple of weeks now, ever since the night he'd watched Johnny Winema back-shoot the Kid and then drag the body into those weeds north of town, Peyt had been trigger-tempered as a treed bobcat.

A feeling of guilt, he supposed, always played havoc with a man's disposition. Several times during the past few days he had flown off the handle at his crew without provocation. He knew Ruth had guessed there was something troubling him, although she had tactfully refrained from speaking of it.

Peyt glanced at the men under Bergendahl's awning. They were obviously riffraff. Their interest in him, he supposed, stemmed partly from envy, for he knew that his tailor-made clothes and this expensive buggy in which he was sitting would mark him down in their book as a man of means.

Ignore them, Peyt thought. And he was doing a good job of that when the door of Horace Pettingill's law office opened and Frank Buckmaster ambled out onto the board-walk.

Frank raised a meaty hand to his hatbrim, curling it down over his eyes, shading them from the morning's bright sunlight. At sight of the big, self-satisfied Broken Bit owner, Peyt felt a swift repugnance, and he looked away. But Frank had spotted him sitting there in the buggy, and now the big man came along the planks toward him.

Frank flung one indifferent glance at the four men under Bergendahl's awning, then ducked under the tie rail and climbed up into the buggy beside Peyt.

"Peyt," he said in a voice that discouraged eavesdropping, "I been wanting to have a talk with you."

Peyt stared fixedly at the buggy's dashboard, not quite trusting himself to look Frank in the eye. "Oh? What about, Frank?"

"Neil Ashton," Frank said, and his voice hardened. "I've put up with about as much from that cocky son as I'm goin' to. I guess you heard he's been tryin' to pin a murder charge on Johnny Winema."

Peyt's mouth was dry, suddenly, and he swallowed. Feeling an utter hypocrite, he said, "Is that right, Frank?"

Frank glanced puzzledly at him, and then nodded. "Damn near anybody," he said, "could have killed that fool Kid. He was always full of big talk and back sass, you know that. You take a chesty little punk like that—sooner or later, the way I look at it, he's bound to find a taker and stop a bullet."

Peyt kept his eyes down on the dashboard of the buggy. You ordered him killed, you big fourflusher, he thought. Who do you think you're kidding? But he only thought it. He didn't say it to Frank.

He was sitting there in sweaty confusion, wondering what tack he ought to take with Frank, when activity down the street pulled at his attention. Lena Le Bon had just emerged from the dressmaker's shop down there, and she came up the plank walk now, her well-developed breasts jiggling noticeably under the flimsy material of her light summer dress.

Peyt watched her as she neared the buggy. She gave the four men under Bergendahl's awning one intensely interested glance, he noticed, and they, in their turn, eyed Lena's figure with a wicked attention.

It angered Peyt, as it would any decent man, and his mouth went thin. But then his hand rose automatically to the brim of his fawn-gray Stetson as Lena smiled him a greeting.

Frank tipped his hat too, Peyt noticed, and it surprised

him to see the way Frank turned his body on the seat of the buggy in order to follow the girl's progress along the walk.

"Someday," Frank said, with a loose-lipped grin at Peyt, "I'm goin' to do something about that." He nodded in Lena's direction, and Peyt frowned.

"I always thought you had ice water in your veins, Frank."

"There's a bit of fluff that could thaw me," Frank said, still grinning, and something in the way it was said made Peyt feel obscurely unclean. Frank was regarding Peyt thoughtfully, and now he said, "Getting back to Neil Ashton, Peyt, I'd kind of like to know how you feel about him. Guess you know I'm fixing to run him out of this country. How do you stand on that matter?"

"Out of it," Peyt said.

Frank was silent for a moment, regarding him. Frank's bushy brows lowered. "Kind of an interesting attitude, Peyt, for a Bench rancher. Neil's a damn cow thief. Strikes me you've got as much to gain by running him out of these parts as I have. Maybe more." Frank grinned cruelly. "I understand he's been seein' a good deal of Ruth Orr. I guess he's tryin' to stir up old embers."

A wild anger against this big, utterly tactless man welled up inside Peyt, but he reminded himself that there was nothing to be gained by antagonizing a bully. "That's the point, Frank," he said wearily. "I can't afford to side you against Neil Ashton. If I did it would queer me for good with Ruth. It would probably throw her right into his arms."

Frank rubbed at the curve of his chin, thinking about that. "All right," he said at last, "I can see what you mean." His eyes touched Peyt's, bold eyes, biting eyes, demanding. "Just don't forget who's fighting your fight, Peyt, if ever I should come to you wanting a favor." Frank grinned, as if to suggest that that time might come at any moment, and stuck out his hammy hand for Peyt to take.

Peyt's eyes flicked down, and suddenly he was perspiring. He was remembering the night he had stood on Ruth's front porch and coldly refused to shake Neil Ashton's proffered hand. How had he tried to explain that inexcusable rudeness to Ruth? "I'm a little choosy who I shake hands with, Ruth. A man's got to draw the line somewhere."

Peyt looked at Frank's extended hand. Now, if ever, Peyt knew, was the time and place to draw that line. Frank Buckmaster was party to a cold-blooded murder that Peyt had witnessed, and the man was a bold-faced liar to boot.

Damned if I'll shake his hand, Peyt thought. His glance rose to Frank's. Something shriveled in him; something died. He put out his hand and grasped Frank's.

Afterward, when Frank had gone, Peyt sat there on the buggy's seat, wallowing in self-recrimination.

He was still at it minutes later, when Adam Bergendahl came out of the store with a carton of groceries balanced on one skinny, uptilted shoulder. The old man was hurrying along at a bent-kneed gait, eager to be rid of his load. Rounding the tie rack, he deposited Ruth's purchases in the boot of the buggy.

Peyt, meanwhile, had stepped down to the street level. He was ducking under the rack, stepping onto the planks of the boardwalk, as Ruth came from the store.

Ruth had a few afterthought purchases wedged under her arm, and she was fiddling with the clasp of her purse, trying to make it snap shut securely. She dropped one of her purchases—a box of raisins—onto the planks.

Peyt bent down, but one of the four men idling under the awning moved more quickly than Peyt. The fellow picked up the raisins and turned toward Ruth, touching grimy fingers to the brim of a shapeless hat as he offered the box to her.

He was a chunky man, built close to the ground. Shorter even than Ruth, Peyt noticed. There was a raffish gallantry about the fellow that bordered on impudence. Peyt's tone was brittle as he said, "I'll take that, fellow."

The man turned and looked Peyt up and down, his small eyes mirroring a remote humor that ought to have warned Peyt that this was nobody to fool with.

"Maybe," the man said, flicking an amused glance at his three companions, "you're afraid I'll contaminate the lady. Is that it, friend?"

Peyt's handsome face took on an expression of lordly

displeasure. He tried to grab the raisins away from the man, but the man only grinned at him, jerking them back. The fellow was making a game of this for the amusement of his companions, and Peyt could feel temper lash through him.

He had just had a good look at himself, and the view had been distinctly unpleasant. A man who has been forced to a lower opinion of himself is, in some ways, not sane. All reasonableness, all sense of caution drained out of Peyt. He hit the short man.

It was a solid punch to the chin. The short man let go of the raisins and went staggering back against the store window. He struck the glass a jarring blow with a point of one shoulder. The thick glass split with a rasping, ear-punishing sound.

There was a moment of silence, and then Ruth was saying, in a low, startled voice, "Peyt, in the name of heaven—"

"Keep out of this, Ruth," Peyt told her. He was watching the man he had hit. The fellow was rubbing at his chin, where Peyt's knuckles had painted a strawberry welt, and there was still that glinting amusement in the small eyes. It bothered Peyt. The fellow seemed almost pleased about what had happened.

Adam Bergendahl had stepped up on the planks, and for a moment the old storekeeper stood with his hands on his aproned hips, contemplating his ruined window. He turned and cocked his head reprovingly at Peyt. His expression was sad rather than angry.

"Peyt," he said, "that glass set me back eighteen dollars. I expect—"

"I'll pay you for it, Adam," Peyt said, and waved the old man to silence.

The man he had hit had pushed away from the window now, and there was something portentous in the little hitch he gave to his shoulders. "That ain't all you'll pay for, friend," he said almost pleasantly, and Peyt knew then that this little man intended to try to finish what he himself had started.

Already a crowd was beginning to gather, the word of a fight having run along the street like wildfire. Ruth, Peyt

65

saw, was embarrassed. It was apparent in her high color, and she had a right to be embarrassed, Peyt decided ruefully.

It was beginning to dawn on him now that he had let temper embroil him in a ridiculous situation, and he swung out savagely at his sawed-off adversary, wanting this stupid affair over with quickly.

The short man's head moved away from his flying knuckles as if it were mounted on rubber. There was something cruelly malicious, Peyt felt, in the way the short man grinned at him. It put him in mind, somehow, of a cat about to entertain itself with a captive mouse; and then things started to happen to Peyt, with soul-shattering swiftness.

The short man came forward, still grinning, and flicked a fist toward Peyt's face. Peyt's hands went up. He realized belatedly, when he was not struck in the face, that the blow had been only a feint, to pull his guard up. He had the impression of being kicked three times in the pit of the stomach.

Peyt knew it was only the short man's fists burying themselves in his flabby midsection, but a mule, he thought sickly, couldn't kick a man much harder than this man could hit.

He let out a sick "Ugh-h-h," and now his hands dropped away from his face. The pain in his stomach had jackknifed him, bringing his head down within range of the small man's knee, which came up swiftly now, to crash against Peyts forehead.

It straightened Peyt up and he caught a heavy blow on the point of the chin. His teeth clicked and ground together and there was a viselike pressure against the top of his head. He reached out in panic, trying to grapple with his opponent, but he was a sick man, blinded by pain, literally helpless.

He felt something wedge itself solidly against his abdomen, and knew it was the small man's shoulder. He was being hoisted aloft then, and carried. Somewhere he heard a man, among the crowd that had gathered to watch, growl out a hurried protest. A woman's involuntary scream came to him like an imagined sound, like something in a dream.

The next thing he was aware of was that he was hurtling through space. He came up against something that offered brief resistance, then gave way with a horrible crash and clatter.

He had just enough consciousness left to realize what it was that was making that awesome racket. Splintering glass.

He had an instant in which to reflect that when he landed he would be on public display, inside Adam Bergendahl's window. An object of mirth, he thought, and then his head banged against something, hard, and there was nothing more to remember.

Chapter Nine

ONE LOOK at the four men under Bergendahl's awning was enough to convince Lena Le Bon that these were Neil's hired hardcases, arrived in town sooner than they'd been expected. They hadn't impressed her.

They'd had a ratty, mean look about them. Now, on her way out Second Street to the wagon yard where she'd left her carriage, Lena remembered how Neil had rejected her suggestion that he become her father's partner, and she was more convinced than ever that he'd been a fool in refusing the offer.

She'd practically proposed marriage to him. She was angry now at the memory of it.

The anger was still working in her minutes later as she trundled along the street in the carriage. Who did Neil Ashton think he was, anyway, to be turning down the best catch in this country?

It was time, Lena thought, that Neil learned his place. All he had in the world was a ranch and a bad reputation, and his hold on the ranch was uncertain.

"He'll wind up working for wages," Lena said through her clenched teeth, "if he doesn't soon come to his senses."

She had clip-clopped along about a mile and a half when

the sound of a horseman rattling along the road behind her pulled her around on the seat of the carriage.

It was Frank Buckmaster, Lena saw, and she frowned, wondering if Frank had followed her out here from town by coincidence or by design.

There was something unsettling in the way Frank's eyes roved over her figure as he pulled his loose-coupled dun up alongside the carriage. Not that Lena particularly minded. She'd put in enough hours at her mirror to know she was a beautiful girl, and she secretly enjoyed being ogled.

"Drivin' home, are you?" Frank asked. His horse was keeping pace with the carriage's progress.

Lena nodded sparingly.

"Your old man," Frank said, "ought to have his head examined. You're too big a girl, Lena, and a sight too good-lookin', to be traipsin' around these hills unescorted. Even in the daytime."

Lena felt a smug satisfaction. In a way, this, her first taste of Frank's heavy-handed gallantry, was the ultimate tribute to her attractiveness. According to the street-corner know-it-alls in Piperock, Frank never looked at a girl. So, at any rate, went the theory. Lena couldn't help smiling, thinking how the glint in Frank's eye now gave that lie to that notion.

"Pull that team in a minute, Lena."

He had a way of tricking you into obeying before you took time to reflect that he had no authority, really. Lena tugged at her reins.

"Yes, sire." There was coquettishness in the smile she directed at him. She was curious about that glint in Frank's eye; she wanted to know what lay behind it.

"I'll drive you home," Frank said in his arrogant, bullish way. He climbed down off his horse and tied it to the back of the carriage. He stepped up to the seat beside Lena, taking her reins. "Tell you the truth," he said, "I been wanting to have a heart-to-heart talk with your father."

"Oh?" Lena said. "What about?"

"Neil Ashton." Frank was staring along the road, and his mouth clamped shut on Neil's name. He was silent a moment; then: "This may interest you, Lena, you bein' a

68

woman. Neil's been tryin' to worm his way back into Ruth Orr's good graces. I reckon you know they used to be sweet on each other."

Lena had known, but she had assumed that old romance was dead, and couldn't possibly be revived, inasmuch as Ruth and Peyt English were said to have an understanding. She glanced sharply at Frank, wondering why he'd bothered to tell her about this. There was no way he could know of her personal interest in Neil.

"Why should it interest me, Frank?" she asked.

"If Neil's allowed to stick around on this range," Frank said, "he'll mess up Ruth's life for her, sure as shootin'. Peyt English is a good-lookin' man, and the girl that marries him won't have to worry where her next party dress is to come from, I don't reckon. I'd hate to see Neil Ashton come between Ruth and Peyt now, and spoil Ruth's chance to be happy. Ruth Orr's had a pretty rough time, so far."

Why, you big faker, Lena thought, you don't care a jot for what happens to Ruth.

Nor do I, she thought grimly. Her heart had jolted at Frank's first linking of Neil's name with Ruth's, and now, in a sort of delayed reaction, a hot jealousy swept her.

Frank was watching her with a shrewd speculation, as if he were trying to guess her thoughts.

"I still intend to run Neil Ashton off Stirrup and out of this country," he stated. "I figured your father and I'd better have an understanding about that."

Lena wasn't listening. It was clearer, now, why Neil had rejected her offer. For the first time in her pampered life Lena was being deprived of something she desperately wanted, and she was caught in the grip of a sulky anger.

If I can't have Neil, Ruth isn't going to, she thought. She looked up at Frank and said coolly, deliberately, "Did you notice those four hard-looking men in front of Bergendahl's when I passed you and Peyt, Frank?"

Frank, alerted by something in her voice, glanced down curiously at her. "I noticed them. What about them?"

"Neil's out home with Dad now," Lena said without hesitation. "He's buying four saddle horses. I understand the four men in town came in by train, from up north. Figure it out for yourself, Frank."

Frank was rubbing the knuckles of one huge hand into the calloused palm of the other. He was silent for so long that Lena was afraid he hadn't heard what she'd said, or hadn't got the idea.

"He's bringing in gunmen, Frank. Don't you see? You'd better get into town and do something about those four men before Neil contacts them."

Frank sat there on the seat of the carriage with his eyes half shut. Then he dropped a suspicious glance toward Lena. "What's your angle?" he asked. "Why are you telling me this?"

"I don't like the idea of his bringing gunmen into a decent, civilized country," Lena lied glibly. "As far as I'm concerned, this range can do without his sort."

Frank sat staring at her for a while. Lena met his glance boldly, and Frank's eyes were puzzled. Quite obviously he hadn't expected to uncover the soul of a censor in one so young and so pretty. He climbed down presently, untied his horse from the rear of the carriage, and lifted himself to the saddle.

Something in the way he thouched his hat and murmured his thanks made Lena feel that she was no longer an attractive girl to Frank, but only an informant.

She watched him ride back toward town, raising a dust cloud, and now the thought of what she had done to Neil began to depress her.

But he'll never know I betrayed him, she thought. Certainly Frank's not going to tell him.

As she reached for the reins she was smiling.

Chapter Ten

INGRAINED CAUTION and a vague hunch that he was riding into trouble made Neil forsake the road on his way into town with the four horses he had bought from Lena's father.

He came up into Piperock from the south side, the four

70

horses trailing behind him on lead ropes. Crossing the railroad tracks, he remembered that Ruth had a wagon shed behind her house, and it occurred to him that he could leave the four horses there.

That way, the town would not have to know he was expecting company. Which was just as well, Neil thought, smiling grimly.

Ruth was in her kitchen, by the window, and she saw him as he threaded the cinder alley that skirted the back of her lot. She came out to greet him as he pulled up alongside her shed, and there was something peculiar in the way she stared at the four horses.

"So that's it," she said.

Neil looked puzzledly at her. She told him about the four strangers in town, about the set-to Peyt had had with the smallest of them.

"Peyt's down at the doctor's, under a sedative now," Ruth said. "He was cut pretty badly. . . . Are those your men, Neil? Is that why you've brought in these four horses?"

"They must've come in on the morning train," Neil said wearily. "I didn't expect them so soon, Ruth."

He could tell, from the way the blue eyes had clouded, that she hadn't liked what she'd seen of his four recruits, and that she was worried for him.

"You'd better hurry uptown, Neil," she said after a moment.

"Why?"

"Your new men are in the Crescent, drinking. Frank seems to have found out somehow who they are and what they're here for. One of my boarders just came in from uptown a minute or two before you got here. He says Frank's trying to talk Roy Millership into arresting your men."

Neil swore savagely under his breath. "Arrest them? What for?"

Ruth smiled commiseratively at him. "That little one did throw Peyt through Adam Bergendahl's window, Neil," she reminded him.

Neil looked at her with affection. Ruth didn't approve of these men he'd brought in, but she was dead loyal. She wasn't going to let Frank steal a jump on him if she could help it.

"Thanks, Ruth," he said.

He left her then, hurrying along the cinder alley and turning into a cross alley that brought him up behind the Crescent. He dismounted hurriedly, tying the gray horse in the shade of a ramshackle building.

There was a back door to the saloon that wasn't much used. Neil approached it with caution. He let himself quietly into the building and found himself in a little anteroom partitioned off from the main part of the saloon.

He could hear voices out front in the big room, where the bar was. He poked his head around the doorjamb and winced at what he saw.

He hadn't got here an instant too soon.

Bat Gardner and three men Neil had never seen before were standing with their backs to the bar, their hands lifted over their heads. Frank Buckmaster, posted at the near end of the bar, was holding a gun on the four, and so was Roy Millership, who stood near the saloon's swing doors.

There was no sign of the bartender, nor was anyone else visible in the long room with its mingled odors of mouldering sawdust, coal oil, whisky, and beer.

Bat Gardner, Neil saw, was staring at Piperock's skinny marshal with a sort of amused contempt in his eyes.

"What's the charge, mister?" he asked, refusing to address the marshal by his title. Roy Millership would have answered, but Frank Buckmaster beat him to it.

"We're taking you boys in on a peace warrant," he said. "If you think you can drift into this town and chuck a respected ranching man through a plate-glass window, you've got another think coming. We're going to make an object lesson of you men."

Bat Gardner pivoted slowly to look at Frank. Bat was an unshaven runt with a look of weasel meanness about him. His uncanny ability to mop up the street with much heavier men in hand-to-hand brawling had made him a sort of living legend up in the Big Horn country, and his skill with a gun had earned him comparison with Bill Hickok.

72

"Who the hell are you?" he asked Frank, and Frank nodded in the marshal's direction.

"He just deputized me before we came in here, friend."

Roy Millership was watching Neil's four recruits at the bar with a steady, careful attention. He said without moving his eyes, "You can take up the collection now, if you will, Frank."

"Sure," Frank said, and he moved along the bar toward the four, grinning.

From where he stood at the rear of the long room, with only his head poked out through the anteroom's doorway, Neil could see Bat Gardner's small, iron-hard body stiffen, and it worried him. He knew that little man, knew there was never any way of predicting Bat Gardner's behavior in this kind of situation.

Frank must have seen something in the small man's eyes that disturbed him, for he halted short of Bat Gardner.

Neil stepped out into the room with his gun in his hand, saying almost idly, "Maybe we'd better skip the collection today, Frank."

Frank whirled at the sound of Neil's voice, a reaction Neil had not anticipated. Frank's gun came around too, arcing toward Neil.

Neil's response to that danger was automatic. He shot almost without taking aim. There was the wicked sound lead makes when it strikes harder metal, and Frank let go of his gun as if it were on fire. It hit the saw-dusted floor and skidded, while the sound of Neil's shot reverberated within the long room.

Frank was cursing, shaking his stinging fingers. It was enough to distract Roy Millership's attention for an instant, and that was all the opening Bat Gardner required. The little man's hand slapped down against the butt of his gun. He brought his leg up, shooting through holster leather.

Roy Millership, hit high in the right arm, was spun by the impact. He dropped his gun, and now, with a composure Neil couldn't help admiring, the marshal regarded Bat Gardner.

"You'll regret that."

"Maybe," Bat said, "you'd of liked it better if I'd put a hole in that tin badge you're wearin', Skinny."

Neil said angrily, "That's enough, Bat." He glanced at Millership, a deep shame washing through him. "Roy, I'm sorry about this. It's too bad it had to happen."

Millership curled the fingers of his left hand around the hurt arm, stanching the flow of blood. "These your men?" he asked.

Neil nodded. "I'm taking them out to Stirrup with me now," he said with quiet determination.

Roy Millership was looking at Frank in swift anger. To Neil it was obvious that the marshal was just beginning to realize how he had been made use of by Frank.

"Frank," Roy said, "I never liked being tricked into carrying wood to another man's fire."

Frank, too shrewd to bluster when he hadn't the cards, shrugged his huge shoulders. Millership, still holding his injured arm, spoke to Neil.

"Get these hoodlums out of my town, understand?"

Neil nodded. "Come on, boys," he murmured, but Bat Gardner was studying the marshal, and didn't move.

"Nobody calls me a hoodlum," Bat said. "I don't stand for it."

"You heard me, Bat," Neil said. He ground out the words.

Bat Gardner glanced at him, then grinned, turning away from Millership with a contemptuous shrug.

Neil herded Bat and his three companions out through the rear of the building. He untied the gray horse, leading the animal along the alley, and he eyed Bat Gardner covertly now, beginning to wonder about the man.

He'd had only a nodding acquaintance with Bat Gardner up north. He'd known Bat was hard as gun metal, and that he was for hire, but he had not known he wore such a big chip on his shoulder.

In one reckless instant, by shooting Piperock's popular marshal, Bat Gardner had destroyed whatever good will Neil might have earned for himself since his return to this country. Frank, Neil knew, would make all he could of what had happened in the Crescent.

74

"Who are your friends, Bat?" Neil murmured after a moment.

Bat introduced them. Their names meant nothing to Neil. They were unkempt, hard-visaged men, with that indefinable stamp of the gun about them. Seeing them here in Piperock, a respectable, workaday town of shops and small houses, he found them less attractive than he otherwise might have done.

These were the kind of men he'd thought nothing of standing up to a bar with during his first years up north. These men epitomized the life he had put behind him. Looking at them now, seeing himself as he might have been, he felt a heady sense of relief, and a gnawing discomfort that he was unable to fathom.

"Where'd you boys leave your saddles?" he asked, and Bat Gardner said: "They're down on the depot platform."

Neil nodded. It didn't take long then to pick up the four horses from under Ruth's shed, and the saddles from the depot. They were rattling out of town in a matter of minutes. Neil felt a lot more comfortable after they'd put Piperock well behind them, and he said so.

"What's worrying you?" Bat Gardner asked idly.

Neil gave the man a thumbnail sketch of the situation between him and Frank. "It's my hunch Frank wants my water and grass, although I haven't been able to prove it. . . . That was a fool thing you did in town just now, Bat, shooting the marshal. Puts me in worse odor around here than I have been. That stunt of chucking Peyt English through a plate-glass window won't help me, either."

"I'm still askin' you what you're worried about," Bat said, shrugging.

"Frank," Neil said. "He'll figure he's got public opinion solidly with him now. He'll uncork a real punch, if I know him."

"Such as?"

"If I knew what kind of punch he intended to throw," Neil said wearily, "I could figure some way to block it. All I know is he won't wait to hit at me now. He won't pull this punch, either."

"That being the case," Bat Gardner said, with a knowing

grin at his three companions, "maybe you and I better have a little talk about money."

Neil frowned at the man. "All right," he said quietly, and the dickering started as they rode along.

Bat Gardner was no blushing violet. He began by asking for five hundred a month for each man. Neil laughed at the outlandish demand.

"Are you crazy? I haven't got a dime from the estate yet. I paid cash for four horses this morning. Where would I get that kind of money?"

Bat muttered. His companions put in their two cents' worth, but when the bargaining ended at last, hours later and within sight of Stirrup buildings, they had settled for one-fifty apiece, which was the figure Neil had had in mind to begin with.

The dickering, with four brains and four tongues racked up against him, had left Neil curiously tired. In Stirrup's yard, introducing the new men to Bill Marion and the rest of the bunch he'd inherited along with the ranch, he was only vaguely conscious of a stiff antagonism between Bat Gardner and his foreman.

Because he had Bill Marion's grudging approval of the plan to bring in these gunmen, Neil felt sure the redhead would make an effort to get along with Bat Gardner and his three sidekicks. So when Marion and Bat Gardner started a conversation, going through motions of civility towards each other, Neil's fears relaxed.

Leaving the two groups of men to get better acquainted, telling himself there was safety in numbers, he sauntered across the yard to the office.

He sat down at the big desk that had once been his father's, and closed his eyes, his body relaxing. The sound of someone's angry cursing across the yard roused him. He had a hunch what to expect, and he went back outside.

He went across the yard and into the bunkhouse, shaking his head with a weary acceptance of bad luck. He found Bat Gardner and Bill Marion squared off at each other in the center of the long room. Bill Marion's freckled face was as red as his hair, and his hands were clenched. Bat Gardner looked cool, and he was grinning, enjoying this, Neil suspected.

Bat's three saddle partners had fanned out behind him, giving him moral support, while the rest of Neil's original crew had taken up similar positions behind the redheaded foreman.

"What's it about, Bat?" Neil asked, and his voice snapped, for he knew that men who can't get along among themselves make poor allies in a range war.

"This ramrod of yours," Bat said, without removing his grinning glance from Bill Marion's face, "needs to be cut down a peg. I told him I always sleep next to a window. He tells me the only two bunks by the windows are taken."

Neil scowled. He might have guessed it was some such triviality that had started the ruckus. Eying Bat Gardner, Neil suspected that the small man had invented a desire to sleep by a window as a pretext to cook up some excitement.

"Bill's right, as you can see for yourself, Bat. Both window bunks *are* taken."

"He's going to have to prove it to me," Bat said.

"No," Neil said, his tone brittle, "he isn't."

Bill Marion's face turned even redder. "I'll handle this, Neil," he said tightly.

"Go ahead," Bat said, taunting him with a grin. "Let's see how you'll handle it, sonny."

Bill Marion couldn't take that. He ran at Bat, launching a roundhouse blow. The small man, fighting dirty, ducked and kicked the redhead on the knee.

The pain crippled Marion for an instant. Gardner, grinning happily, was about to pour lefts and rights into the foreman's body when Neil came down the floor in three reaching strides and caught the man by his bandanna.

He dragged the little man back, off his balance. The knot gouging at his Adam's apple made Bat Gardner's breath rasp. He turned on Neil, the killing rage of an aroused animal flashing into his eyes.

Neil faced the man, his narrowed eyes daring Bat to start something. The wild anger in the small man subsided, but his voice was sullen as he said, "You're makin' a habit of spoilin' my fun. I'm gettin' tired of it."

77

Neil was thinking of Frank as he murmured, "You'll have all the fun you can stomach in a matter of hours, unless I'm mistaken. Just stick around."

Bat glared at him, but didn't say anything. Neil debated. He had succeeded in diverting Bat's attention from Bill Marion for the time being, but the instant he left the bunkhouse the quarrel would probably be picked up again.

Neil said reluctantly, "You and your boys follow me, Bat."

"What for?"

"I'm bunking you down in the house. There's room for you up there."

Bat Gardner and his three sidekicks exchanged grins, and Bat threw a triumphant glance at Neil's redheaded foreman. Hired gunmen don't normally rate soft beds in the boss's house.

There was a victory, of sorts, for Bat Gardner in the arrangement. Neil saw the disgruntlement in Bill Marion's eyes, and wondered bitterly how long he could keep these two groups of men at Stirrup.

Not long, he decided, and it came to him that he might have made a tragic blunder in recruiting Bat and his three hardcase companions.

Chapter Eleven

NEIL SHOOK HIS HEAD wearily and threw down his hand, an open-end straight that he had failed to fill. He leaned back in his chair, contemplating these new men of his as they bet their cards and built up the pot in the center of the table.

They had fallen into the listless attitudes of men to whom the game of poker is less a battle of wits than a test of endurance. They'll play till dawn, Neil thought.

He glanced up at the wall clock, and saw that it was past midnight. He waited until the hand was played out, then pushed away from the table and rose, yawning and stretching his arms.

"I'm bushed and I'm hungry," he said. "If you boys want something to eat before you turn in, you can come along with me to the kitchen."

All four of his recruits grinned at the mention of food. They fell in eagerly behind Neil as he crossed the room toward the door at its far end.

Neil was almost out of the room when it happened. Passing the window he heard the raspy sound of a bullet biting its way through glass. The slug whipped through the cloth of his coat, missing his ribs by a hair's breadth, and thunked into the masonry wall at the opposite end of the room.

The report of the rifle, a brittle sound muffled by the thick walls, followed closely on the heels of the sniper's bullet. It seemed to come from somewhere on the grass hummocks out behind the house.

Neil whirled away from the window and snapped his gun out of the holster. He was about to throw a shot at the lamp on the table they had used for their poker game when he saw that Bat Gardner's gun was out, already on it.

Bat squeezed the trigger. The lamp splintered and fell to the floor. The room darkened.

For a while then, lead whipped into the building from a half-dozen directions. Neil knelt by the window through which the sneak shot had come. He knocked the pane out with the muzzle of his gun, and watched the action out there on the grass hummocks.

Counting the gun flashes, he soon realized that this was a full-scale raid; this was Frank's answer to what had happened today in the Crescent.

Neil shot at muzzle flame out there on the grass. His erstwhile poker opponents had stationed themselves at the room's two side windows, and were returning the raiders' fire.

Neil heard muffled firing from inside the dark bunkhouse. Bill Marion and the others of the original crew were doing that shooting, he realized, and he wondered suddenly what Frank hoped to accomplish here.

This fight had to end in a stalemate, unless Frank tried

to burn them out of these buildings, and Neil didn't think Frank was ready for that yet.

It occurred to Neil that whoever had shot at him through the window had definitely attempted to kill him. Maybe that was all Frank had hoped to accomplish.

The thought of it put an edge on his temper. One man out on the grass, he saw, was firing steadily at the house. After pin-pointing the sniper's position and considering the angle at which the bullet had entered the room, Neil was reasonably certain he'd located the man who had tried to get him.

He posted one of the others at this window, with orders to keep the man out on the grass busy. He hurried along the dark hall to the kitchen, and let himself out the panty door into a pool of shadow.

There was only a short stretch of yard between the door of the pantry and the screening tall grass of the hummocks. He crawled as far as the grass on his hands and knees, then dropped into a narrow gully.

Neil had played stalk-the-Injun here as a boy. He knew every twist and turn of this gully. He worked his way cautiously along it, swinging out into the hummocks and around to a position behind the man who had tried for him.

He poked his eyes up above the lip of the gully and saw a man flattened against the ground behind a small hillock, aiming a rifle at the house. There was just enough moonlight to let him make out the dark, vague shape against the ground, but not enough to permit recognition.

Carefully now, holding his six-gun in front of him, Neil eased his body past the lip of the gully onto flat ground. He crawled toward the fellow.

It came to him that if he could take this man alive, it might be possible to scare him into doing some talking. A man afraid of his life is an unpredictable quantity, Neil knew. The wild hope surged up in him, as he inched his way forward, that he might somehow induce the man to sell Frank out to the sheriff.

I've got to take him alive, he thought. I've got to do it.

He was less than ten yards from the man now. He kept snaking forward, the drought-stricken grass crackling like hay under the weight of his body. It sounded to Neil like the beating of a hundred miniature drums. It amazed him that the man he was stalking did not hear it.

He had come up within eight yards of his man, and was resting a moment, his head pinned to the ground, when he heard the sound.

It was the sound of a man's heavy footfalls. It was telegraphed to him very clearly, and it grew louder as he listened, indicating that the man making that sound was coming in this direction.

Neil swore, realizing his luck had run out. It would be only a matter of seconds before his presence here was discovered. He lined his gun on the man lying prone behind the low hillock, but could not bring himself to press the trigger.

Scowling at his own weakness, he wormed his way backward, trying to reach the comparative safety of the gully before the other man came up within eyeshot of him.

A shadowy figure loomed up suddenly from behind a sharp rise off to Neil's right, and for an instant the figure struck a statue-like pose. Neil knew the man had seen him laying on the ground.

"Joe?" the man's voice called softly, and the answer came from the man Neil had been stalking.

"Over here."

The man atop the rise shot at Neil then without hesitation. The bullet passed through the crown of Neil's hat, nudging it back off his forehead. The muzzle of Neil's gun lifted and he shot the man through the body, knocking him down, and then whipped his glance around at the man he'd been stalking.

He heard a low grunt, and saw that the fellow was swinging the rifle around toward him.

Neil cocked his six-gun with a slapping motion of his left hand, and squeezed out a quick shot at the man. The slug must have taken him in the lungs, for he let out a gurgling scream and rolled back, his legs writhing, his whole body thrashing.

"Joe? Joe?" The voice came from a point a hundred yards distant, and Neil recognized it as Frank's. In a few moments Frank would be over here to find out why his hail had not been answered, or he would send someone to scout the situation.

Neil rolled back into the gully and stumbled along it, heading back toward the ranch house. Just before he reached the yard he heard Frank curse wildly behind him.

Frank, it appeared, had discovered the two dead men Neil had left out there on the grass. Neil could hear the big man grinding out guttural orders. He couldn't make out what Frank was saying, but presently he saw a single Broken Bit rider charge in recklessly toward the Stirrup buildings.

Frank and the rest of his crew were giving this reckless fellow covering fire, and Neil noticed that the man was wheeling his horse first one way and then the other, making a difficult target by moonlight for the men in the house and the bunkhouse.

Neil watched the man swing off behind Stirrup's barn and strike a match to a pile of hay. The hay abutted the barn; if it burned, the barn would burn with it, Neil thought, cursing, and he snapped a shot at the fellow.

The range was too great for accurate work with a pistol. He watched the flame lick its way up through the hay now as the man wheeled and leaped back to his saddle.

The man was lighted up beautifully for an instant by the fire he had set. Someone let go at him with a Winchester from inside the bunkhouse. The man's body jolted, then went limp. He clutched at the horn with both hands, trying desperately to stay in the saddle.

The motion of his horse pitched him off to one side. As he fell, his foot twisted and was caught in the stirrup. The horse dragged him along the ground for a couple of steps and then stopped, refusing to drag the man farther.

Flames were eating their way up along the barn wall now. Neil fought down a foolhardy impulse to dash over there and try to put out the fire. He had no desire to commit suicide by making a target of himself for Frank and his men.

The barn was doomed, and he watched it with a sort of dismal acceptance, at the same time thanking his stars there was no livestock inside the flaming building.

An ever widening circle of light was flung out across the grass by the high-reaching flames. Neil stared steadily toward the position from which Frank's voice had reached him, but Frank and his men must have retreated as swiftly as the light strengthened, for he saw no sign of them anywhere.

After a moment Neil heard a clatter of horses' hoofs on gravel.

Frank and his crew, Neil knew then, had had enough of the battle and were riding out.

Neil crossed the yard to the house. Rounding the corner of the buildings, he saw that the Broken Bit rider who had set the fire had somehow unsnagged his foot from the stirrup and had crawled over here, away from the heat of the burning barn.

Neil drew his gun and approached the man, who sat on the ground in a sort of glaze-eyed misery. The man didn't move, seemed hardly aware of what was happening, as Neil leaned down and eased his gun quickly from the holster.

Neil heard the door of the house open behind him, and then light footfalls approaching. Bat Gardner was standing beside him then, contemplating the hurt man on the ground with the ruthlessness of a preying animal that had made a capture.

"What'll we do with him?" Bat asked, glancing at Neil. "Shoot him?"

The man on the ground cocked his head a little and looked at Bat with the brightness of fear in his eyes. He had taken part in the raid and had fired the barn, and he seemed to realize as he studied Bat Gardner's ferret face that he could expect no mercy.

Seeing that fear in the man, Neil decided to let this situation develop, on the chance that the man's tongue might start wagging.

Bat's three sidekicks had come out of the house to watch the fun, and Bill Marion and the rest of the gang from the bunkhouse were on their way across the yard now, Neil noticed.

Bat was still waiting for an answer to the question he'd asked. Neil gave a careless little shrug, as if to say, "Suit yourself. I don't care what you do with him."

Bat grinned and turned slowly, deliberately, toward the three men who had accompanied him into this country.

"One of you get a rope," he said.

The man on the ground flinched, and glanced toward Neil in a mute plea. Neil met the man's glance without change of expression, then looked coldly away. Bill Marion and the bunkhouse gang, he noticed, were staring at him as though seeing him for the first time.

A rope was brought, and now Bat Gardner coiled it expertly in his left hand and then flipped the end over a low sturdy limb of the cottonwood shading the front of the house. Deliberately then Bat fashioned a noose, while the man on the ground watched with a sort of dull-eyed fascination.

For two full minutes there was no sound other than the fierce popping and crackling of the flames that were eating the heart out of the barn. Bill Marion's face was red with a rising sense of outrage, but Neil managed to get the foreman's eye and communicate to him that he was to stay out of this.

When the noose was almost ready, the man on the ground found his voice. "Y-you ain't goin' to hang me, friend," he said.

"No?" Bat said, and he laughed cruelly. He turned to the man who had fetched the rope and said, "Last I saw of this fire bug's horse, it was standing out on the hummocks. Go get it."

The fellow nodded, and turned away on his errand. The man on the ground watched him go, then looked up at Bat. "I'm hit bad, in the belly. You try to hoist me up on a horse and I won't last long enough to stretch that rope for you, mister. Leave me lay here and die on my own time, why don't you? I ain't done nothing to deserve hanging."

"After we hang you," Bat said, "we're goin' to cut you down and tie you on your horse and let him carry you back where you came from. Maybe when some of your friends see the rope burns on your neck they'll realize it don't pay to come raiding this outfit. Maybe some of them will high-tail it out of the country."

The man on the ground looked at Neil again, and Neil felt all these men looking at him, wondering what had held him silent so long.

Bat said, "Any objections?" and Neil flicked a covert glance at the man on the ground.

"No objections," he said, and he saw the surprised disbelief in Bill Marion's eyes. He gave the redhead a little shake of the head, a mute warning to be silent. Bat Gardner was motioning to his three partners, ordering them to lift the Broken Bit man up onto his horse.

A wild fear came into the man's eyes, and Neil decided this was the psychological moment.

"If you wanted to talk a little, my friend," he said, "you might not have to put on the rope dance."

The man's eyes came up, bright with a quick hope. "Talk about what?"

"Who killed the kid?"

"Winema, probably," the man said. "I couldn't swear to it, though. Nobody at Broken Bit's talking much about it."

Neil swore. He had not anticipated that Frank and Winema would be so careful. This man's imperfect testimony would not impress Sheriff Tobe Hendy.

Bat Gardner's blood lust was aroused. He said impatiently, "He can't tell you nothing. Let's get it over with."

"We're not going to hang the man, Bat," Neil announced quietly.

The small man stared at him. "You change your mind kind of sudden. A minute ago you said—"

"That was a minute ago," Neil said. There was no point, he supposed, in explaining why he'd pretended to approve of what Bat had planned for this poor devil. "You can lift him up on his horse, boys," Neil said, "and then we're letting him ride out of here."

"What's the idea?" Bat shouted.

"He may not make it back to Broken Bit with that hole in his belly," Neil said, "but where he falls off the horse is where someone will find him. And there won't be any marks of a rope on him, Bat."

"You're a fool," Bat said. "You're fighting a man who's out to kill you, who's willing to shoot at you through a window. You capture one of his men, and you're turnin' him free to come at you again. That ain't my kind of fighting."

"Lift him up on his horse, boys," Neil said, ignoring the

small man. It occurred to him that Bat's men might be purposely rough with the prisoner, and he waved them away, turning to the foreman. "You and the boys lift him, Bill. Be gentle with him."

They hoisted the hurt man into the saddle, while Bat Gardner, cheated of his victim, scowled. The Broken Bit rider sat there swaying, clutching at the horn, his face gray as flour paste in the wash of pallid yellow light from the blazing barn.

"All right," Neil said, "it's up to you now, friend. Ride out."

The man grinned at him in a sick way, and coughed lightly. His face was even grayer, Neil thought, and then the man said, in a voice so weak Neil could barely make the words out, "Thanks. Thanks. . . . I . . ."

It was the last speech the man uttered. He came pitching down at Neil, no longer able to hold his place in the saddle as internal bleeding choked off his breath. Neil caught the man and eased him down on the ground, and watched him rattle his final few breaths out.

He heard Bat Gardner's low chuckle, and looked up in time to see the man direct a triumphant grin at his three cronies.

The men were amused at the way this situation had worked itself out, Neil knew, and it came to him that there must be something basically rotten at the core of men who took any satisfaction from another man's dying in great pain.

Neil had taken a few drinks with Bat Gardner up north, had sat in poker games with him, and that was the extent of his acquaintance with the man. He had not known Bat's three companions at all, and he was happy now to be able to say that, for he was seeing these men for what they were.

He had not looked for softness in these men. You had no right to look for that trait in professional gunmen. But even a hired gunman must have some strain of decency and loyalty in him, or he is worthless. He could never bind these men to him by any of the normally accepted codes of behavior. These men were not normal. They lived by no code, except perhaps that of self-interest.

86

Neil made his decision.

"You and your boys may as well saddle your horses, Bat," he said.

The small man's head came up sharply. "What for?"

"I made a mistake asking you to come down here," Neil said quietly. "You're no good to me here. I'm not ready to make it that kind of fight."

Bat Gardner accepted it without visible surprise. "You haven't paid me and the boys nothing yet," he reminded him.

"Before you ride out, come up to the office. I'll give each of you expenses plus twenty-five dollars for this night's work, and we'll call the score even."

"That ain't enough," Bat snapped. "We been shot at to-night. When a man lays his life on the line, it's worth more'n twenty-five dollars."

Neil looked at the short man, smiling. "Take it or leave it, Bat," he said mildly.

Bat Gardner didn't say anything, just stood there sullenly.

"When you leave here," Neil said, "ride to Piperock. Drop those horses off at the livery stable. I'll pick them up the next time I get into town."

"Maybe," Bat said, "we'll just hang onto those horses." He grinned. "You always had a good eye for horseflesh. I kind of like the looks of the one I rode up here from the depot."

Neil regarded the man for a moment and asked without rancor, "Have you got a bill of sale for the horse, Bat?" He waited a moment, then added, "Because if you haven't, it might not be safe to ride it out of this country."

"Meanin'?" Bat Gardner asked.

It was Neil's turn to grin. "Somebody might figure you stole the horse, Bat. Especially if I registered a complaint against you with the sheriff's office."

Bat Gardner's eyes held a crazy, wild glint, and his jaw muscles were working. But he only shrugged, nodding toward his three cronies, and walked across the yard toward the corral. It was not at all the reaction Neil had anticipated, and he watched them go, deeply troubled.

Bill Marion came over to stand beside him, and said, "I never did believe there's anything wrong in changing horses in midstream. You did a smart thing. We're well rid of those killers."

Neil was still thinking of the wicked anger he'd seen in Bat Gardner's eyes. It was not Bat Gardner's way to accept a punch without striking back, and Neil shook his head, his worry increasing.

"We're well rid of them," he said, "*if* we're rid of them."

Chapter Twelve

BAT GARDNER rode into Frank Buckmaster's Broken Bit headquarters in the first gray light of dawn. He rode in with his hands held high, holding his horse down to a sedate walk. As further evidence of peaceful intentions, he had removed his gun belt from around his small waist and draped it around the saddle horn.

It would be impossible for him to fill his hand in a hurry. Frank's sentry out by the front gate could see that, so instead of shooting the visitor, he ordered Bat to drop his gun belt to the ground, and then motioned him in toward the ranch buildings.

The Chinese cook roused Frank from heavy sleep, so that he might greet the visitor. Frank's mood, as he stepped out onto the dew-damped patio flagstones, was cranky. He regarded Bat Gardner, who had halted his horse just short of the patio, and was sitting there quietly, as if waiting for an invitation to light down.

"I'll say one thing for you," Frank said. "You've got one hell of a nerve with you, friend."

The bunkhouse gang was awake, sifting out of the low, rectangular building in varying degrees of undress. There were hats, shirts, even a few pairs of boots missing, but every man of the lot had remembered to strap on a gun, Frank saw with a grin.

Johnny Winema came deliberately across the yard and dropped into position a scant twenty feet from the man on the horse. The half-breed's hand was on his gun, and judging from the way he was watching Bat Gardner, he was hoping the man would make a false move.

Frank threw the gunman a glance that said, "Take it easy until we find out what he wants."

Bat Gardner shifted his weight in the saddle, arousing a creak of protest from the leather. "I'm here to smoke the peace pipe," he said, his eyes touching Frank's.

Frank studied the small man's expressionless face before asking, "How come?"

"Me and Neil Ashton," Bat said, "have parted company." His quick grin had no humor in it. "The goodby wasn't said friendly."

Frank tugged at his ear, wondering if this could be some sort of trick. But a glint of anger had come into Bat Gardner's eyes as he spoke Neil Ashton's name, and Frank told himself a reaction like that could hardly be faked.

"How about your three friends?" Frank asked. "Have they quit Ashton too?"

Bat nodded. "Two of them," he said, "are climbin' on a train right about now, down in Piperock. Leavin' these parts for good."

"Two of them," Frank said, his lips pursing, and Bat Gardner said with a wave of his arm, "Other one's back there waitin' for me. If I don't ride out of here alive, he'll see to it my relatives hear about it."

Frank digested that, grinning. "What's on your mind, friend?"

Bat Gardner shook his head. "I ain't much at talking from the saddle. What I've got to say is for your ears, Buckmaster."

Frank's curiosity was aroused. He glanced toward Winema, but decided not to dismiss the gunman.

"Step down," he said to Bat Gardner, and at the same time he motioned to Winema to come closer.

Bat Gardner dismounted and Frank led the way into the office. Winema followed them, watching Bat Gardner every instant. The small man obviously didn't like that, but he made the best of the situation.

He told Frank what had happened at Stirrup after the

raid, editing the facts a bit to make them more palatable to Frank. Bat's temper exploded as he spoke of Neil Ashton's refusal to let him and the boys keep their horses.

"I've got to leave this horse I'm ridin' at the stable in Piperock and buy myself another; otherwise he'll have the law on me for horse stealing. No man can take that tack with Bat Gardner and not damn soon regret it."

This was shaping up, Frank thought. He studied the short man. "How were you figuring to make him regret it, Gardner?"

Bat Gardner shook his head, grinning. "I been wondering what's in this fight for you, friend," he said slyly.

"Have you?"

"After what happened last night," Bat said, "I'd lay odds there's more than a grudge behind your efforts to squeeze Ashton off Stirrup. I'd say you're playin' in a high-stake game, and only you know how much is in the kitty."

Frank smiled. It disturbed him to have this brash little gun-slammer hit the nail on the head so precisely. But Frank's eyes betrayed nothing. "That what you'd say, friend?"

"Maybe," Bat said, "I could help you, Buckmaster, if you'd care to make it worth my while."

"Help me how?" Frank asked slowly.

Bat Gardner shifted his weight from one small leg to the other. He glanced toward Johnny Winema.

"What I have in mind's pretty raw," he said. "It would cost you some money."

"I've got some money," Frank said, studying the man. There was something of the snake in this Bat Gardner, Frank decided. The man made Frank's skin crawl, which was an accomplishment, for Frank rarely felt uneasy in any man's presence.

"It's something I'd rather not talk about in front of a witness," Bat Gardner said, and again his glance swiveled at Winema. "I ain't armed, you can see that," he said, as Frank hesitated.

Frank's lips compressed. He had a feeling that he was not

going to like the man's proposition, whatever it was, but that he would nonetheless buy it.

There was a sort of fatalism in the short nod with which he dismissed Winema.

The barn, fortunately, stood well away from Neil's other buildings, so there was no danger of the fire's spreading. It burned out during the night. A few tendrils of smoke still rose from the wreckage at two-thirty in the afternoon of the day after the raid, when John Llewellyn and Jules Le Bon rode into Stirrup with a group of Neil's ranching neighbors.

Neil greeted them at the head of the lane, asking, "Anything I can do for you, gentlemen?"

John Llewellyn, speaking for the group, said, "Reason we're here is to ask you that question, son."

Neil stared at the silver-haired rancher, not understanding. John Llewellyn nodded toward what was left of Stirrup's barn. "You'll have to get a new building up before cold weather sets in. We figured if we all chipped in and staged an old-fashioned barn raising, we could have her up for you in jigtime."

Neil regarded these men. He had never seen soberer faces, but their eyes reflected that quiet pleasure that comes to men banded together to do a good turn. He had good neighbors, Neil knew, and tautness caught at his chest, making it hard to breathe.

He knew the risk these men ran in coming to him with this offer. Frank would not thank them for siding against him. He would let them know about it, and some of these older ranchers were just independent and salty enough to tell Frank where to head in, Neil thought worriedly.

"Thanks anyway, gents," he said. "I'll manage."

It was easy to see they hadn't anticipated this reaction to their offer, and that they didn't like it.

They left presently, though, wagging their heads. Neil watched them ride out, and then turned to see Bill Marion coming toward him across the yard. Bill wanted to know what the visitors had wanted. He frowned when Neil told him.

"Why didn't you accept their help?" he asked.

"You think I should have?" Neil murmured.

The redhead nodded. "Let a man do you a good turn, and you'll make a friend of him every time. We can use friends on this range, if you ask me. This won't be no tea party now. Not after last night."

Neil stared out over the grass hummocks. "Frank burned that barn, Bill. If I let those fellows chip in to help me put up a new one, we'd wind up with a full-scale range war on our hands. I'd hate to feel I'd been the cause of something like that."

"You said you had a hunch Frank wants you off this place so he can grab it himself, that annexing Stirrup could be his opening gun in a campaign to make himself top dog around here. If that's the case, Frank's got to be stopped, Neil. And it's as much their fight as it is yours."

"That's only my hunch, Bill. I can't prove it. Until I can, I'd rather not drag anyone else into the fracas."

"Don't guess there'd be much point," the redhead admitted, "in draggin' the whole range into it."

Neil said soberly, "What about that gang in the bunkhouse? As you say, this is liable to get pretty rough, after last night. Those fellows don't owe me anything. None of you do, Bill. This thing goes back a long, long way with me and Frank, and—"

"I'll mention it to the boys," the redhead said. "They'll stick. I know those lads, Neil. I know how they feel toward you by this time."

Neil had to look away from the foreman. His cup, he was thinking, had run over now. He had his ranching neighbors, except for Peyt English, with him in spirit in this quarrel with Frank, and he had a crew he could count on.

The redheaded foreman sauntered away, and Neil stayed put, staring out over the grass. There'd still been no rain to break the long siege of dry weather. Peyt English's Sunk Creek outfit was always the first of the outfits up here on the Bench to suffer when rain didn't fall. Sunk Creek had its headwaters in low, sparsely vegetated hills, a poor watershed that permitted rapid runoff.

That was one of the reasons, Neil supposed, that Charlie

Heber had quit trying to grub out a living for himself down there on the Sunk, and had sold out to Peyt English. The more Neil thought about the probable condition of the range down there, the more perturbed he became.

He finally caught up and saddled the gray horse and rode out, telling Bill Marion not to expect him back till after supper.

It was a leisurely two-hour ride from Stirrup down to Peyt English's headquarters. Ordinarily Neil might have enjoyed the trip down there, but coming off green slopes to the broad valley floor, he saw there wasn't even a trickle of water in Sunk Creek's meandering bed, and he shook his head.

Now, as he traveled the floor of the valley, he began to see Peyt English's cattle. They were standing around in scattered bunches, keeping to shade, their heads down, a curious apathy discernible in their postures. Now and again a steer would lift its head and bawl for water, and the sound went through Neil like a lance, for once he had been caught with a dry canteen on the desert, and he knew the brutal suffering prolonged thirst brings.

Riding along roughly parallel with the dry stream bed, he traced the valley out toward its mouth, and rounded a bend that brought him in sight of Peyt English's buildings, which lay in a patternless cluster on a wide curve of the Sunk.

A wire fence surrounded the outfit. The fence was new, but otherwise the place had not changed since Neil had last seen it. He let himself in through the gate and trotted over toward the house.

He reined in abruptly, gaping, as Peyt English came out of the house and pointed a long-barreled Colt's revolver deliberately at him.

There was brittle anger in English's pale eyes, and a rasp in his voice as he said, "Turn that gray around and ride out of here, Ashton, before I blow a hole in you."

Chapter Thirteen

THE GUN in Peyt English's hand was trained on Neil's stomach. There was a wildness in the man's eyes that had a sobering effect on Neil. A gun in the hand of a hysterical fool is nothing to be taken lightly. He was in as ticklish a situation here as he ever had been in.

He stared unbelievingly at English's finger as it applied pressure to the gun's trigger.

"Easy, man," he said in the tone of voice he would use to calm an excitable horse. "You might let me state my business before—"

"Ride out," English snapped.

It came to Neil that this man undoubtedly held him accountable for the humiliation he had suffered at the hands of Bat Gardner in Piperock. It was Neil, after all, who had brought Bat Gardner into this country. But Peyt English had some growing up to do if he could not face the fact that he had invited that trouble with Bat.

Eying the man, Neil gave a mental shake of his head. English, he was beginning to see, was the sort of man who showed to advantage while things were going his way, but who tightened up, turned brittle and mean under pressure.

His camouflage had been good enough to fool Ruth— and Ruth was not easily taken in—but it was only a question of time, Neil reasoned, before she'd have the man's number. Come to think of it, her eyes had probably been opened a little that night Neil had offered English his hand and the fellow had pretended not to see it.

This man really hates me, Neil thought.

"I'm here to offer you the use of my lake water, English," he said quietly. "Some of those critters I saw on the way down here will be buzzard bait in another few days if they aren't watered."

"They're my cattle, Ashton. I'll worry about them."

Neil frowned. "What's between you and me will keep till

94

another day, won't it? Those cows don't enter into our quarrel. I'm offering you a chance to save them."

"And I'm refusing the offer," English said. The gun in his hand steadied. "Now turn around and ride out."

Neil felt a rising impatience. English was carrying pigheadedness a little too far. It was harder, now, to understand what Ruth had thought she saw in this fellow. But there was no denying the man his good looks. He dressed well, and he had that indefinable manner about him that goes with inherited wealth. Then, too, Ruth had known him less than six months. During that brief time English had probably put his best foot forward with her. Even so, there must be some good in the man, Neil decided, if Ruth had considered marrying him. Gambling on it, Neil said: "I'm not riding out, English, until you come to your senses."

One corner of English's mouth twitched, and that wildness came back into his pallid eyes. Neil flinched, realizing this man was undoubtedly capable of pulling the trigger in a fit of anger.

He was wondering whether he ought to wait the situation out, or try to get his own gun out and throw crippling lead into Peyt English, when a voice spoke from the corner of the house.

"I wouldn't do that, boss," the voice said.

Peyt English, thrown off his emotional balance by the interruption, made a flicking turn of his head, just enough to let him glance at the speaker.

Neil glanced over there too. A tall, stringily built puncher had eased around the corner of the building and was leaning against the masonry, contemplating Peyt English.

"You're foreman here," Peyt snapped at the man. "I'm owner. Let's keep that relationship in mind, shall we?"

"Sure." The man nodded. "All the same, if I was you I'd put the gun up. I couldn't help overhearin' what you two was arguing about. It wouldn't go too good for you in court, boss, if you was to shoot Ashton and I told a jury how you come to do it."

"Damn it," Peyt said, "don't mess in this. Take orders."

"I'll take orders when you start actin' like a man that's entitled to give them. You been like a crazy man around

95

here for more'n two weeks. There's a limit to the amount of that a crew'll put up with. I don't mind tellin' you your crew's pretty near reached that limit."

Peyt English's anger seemed to melt away as his foreman talked. He blanched at the prospect of being left crewless. His leveled gun lowered.

The man leaning against the building nodded at Neil, murmuring, "You'd better ride, Ashton. It's no use tryin' to make him see the light. I been harpin' at him about those critters for three days. He just keeps sayin' it'll rain tomorrow, it's got to."

Neil swore under his breath. It angered him to think of dumb animals suffering because of any man's stiff-necked pride. He spoke to Peyt English's foreman.

"Lake water's there, if and when you're ready to use it."

The man nodded warm thanks. English's face had turned red again. Neil realized it infuriated the man that he had been bypassed, that Neil's final offer had been made not to Peyt, but to the foreman.

He'll hate me more now than ever, Neil thought wearily, as he turned the gray horse and rode out.

No rain fell during the week, and Neil waited anxiously for some overture from Peyt English or from his foreman. He could not make himself believe that English would let his animals die, rather than accept the use of Stirrup water.

Bill Marion told him not to worry about it. "I'll give odds something's been done for English's critters by this time. Frank Buckmaster's probably still got some water to spare, although if this drought ain't soon broke by a good rain, he's liable to wind up in the peculiar position of havin' to ask you for the use of lake water, along with the rest of these Bench ranchers. Peyt's probably gone to Frank for help, and paid through the nose for it."

Peyt could afford to pay, Neil supposed. He'd heard that Peyt's father was a millionaire. He quit worrying about Peyt's cattle.

Bill Marion said, "Time we did a little worrying about our own critters. We've got some pretty dry range up in those hills above Hay Creek. Maybe me and one of the boys better take a look up that way."

It occurred to Neil that such a trip could be risky, with Frank and his men on the warpath.

"I'll go," he said idly. "It's a long time since I've had a look at that country up there."

He rode out shortly, refusing to let the foreman ride along with him. Marion didn't like the idea of Neil's riding alone, but when Neil told him to stay put and look after the ranch, there was nothing the redhead could do but shrug and take orders.

It took Neil a couple of hours of alternate trotting and loping to get up into the Hay Creek country. It was a lonely, uninviting section of broken hills, small canyons, and mesas. There was good grass here, but only in patches; the cattle had to rustle for their forage.

Hay Creek itself, he was pleased to discover, still held a small trickle of water. What few Stirrup-branded steers he saw appeared to be in good flesh. It bothered him, though, that he didn't see more of them. It seemed to him that this range could support cattle in greater numbers.

Halting beside a cairn that had been placed by his father to mark one border of the Stirrup graze, he shifted in the saddle, trying to ease his cramped leg muscles.

Low limestone hills lay before him, their rimrocked surfaces glinting brassily in the sun. The reflection was bright enough to sting a man's eyes, if he looked steadily toward it. Glancing down, Neil let his gaze run across a stretch of barren, gravelly ground. He picked out a faint tracing of hoofprints, and frowned.

These prints were of cattle, he saw at a glance, and he judged them to be a day or two old. They swung along the flat for some distance, then slanted upslope, aiming, apparently, at a break in the low hills.

Neil estimated that there must have been about a dozen big steers in the bunch that had gone through here. He picked out the faint but unmistakable prints of two horses, and his mouth twisted.

He had his hunch about this now, and it was something he did not like to think about. For a brief moment he hesi-

97

tated, considering the danger into which he might be riding; then he touched spurs to the gray, following the trail of the cattle and the two horsemen up into the hills.

Whoever had taken the beef, Neil saw, had made a conscientious effort to cover their tracks. He traced the dim, hard-to-read trail out along a flinty ridge, down a ravine, along a dry stream bed that traversed the floor of a shallow valley, and up into another range of low-lying hills.

After several hours of this painfully slow going, he pulled up atop a ridgelike knoll and stared out across a series of mesas. Now, as though the men he followed felt certain no one could have trailed them to this point, the sign became almost ridiculously easy to follow. He pushed on rapidly, making his way up and down hogbacked rises.

Topping one of these, he drew rein at sight of a band of antelope grazing in a little park under a canopy of trees. For an instant the animals stood at attention, watching him with startled bright eyes; then they wheeled like soldiers on parade and glided away.

Neil watched them, smiling, until they were out of sight. He pushed on, crossing a tableland several miles wide, and lost the trail of the cattle finally as he clattered out onto high rimrock overlooking a scene that held him motionless in the saddle.

Beneath him lay an enormous depression, a giant saucer carved out of the earth. One sheer rock wall ran almost to the North Platte River. Southward the rimrock traced out a rough crescent, with tiny gulches knifing down through it.

The beef, Neil assumed, had been driven down to the lower level by way of one of these gulches. This was Goshen Hole he was looking into. Bench cattle had a way of wandering in here, he had heard, and disappearing as completely as though swallowed by quicksand.

From this high vantage point the view was one of almost unbelievable beauty, but what caught and held his attention was movement off to his left at the base of the cliff, where some buzzards, having found carrion to feed on, were flapping wings over their feast and squalling at one another.

The face of the cliff shouldered out between him and

the birds, so that he could not see what they fed on. He pulled the gray horse back, away from the rimrock, and turned the animal in that direction.

Nearing the cliff beneath which he had seen the birds feeding, he caught the stench of something dead and unburied. He dismounted, leaving the gray in the shade of a niggardly cluster of piñons, and, curiosity driving him, walked to the cliff's edge and peeked cautiously over.

What he saw was enough to make his insides roll over sickly. There was a jumble of jagged-edged rocks at the foot of the cliff, and Stirrup-branded cattle—dozens of them—had been hazed over the rim to be broken and gutted when they hit bottom.

There were more buzzards down there than Neil had realized. The birds were having themselves a field day. Some of them were so glutted they seemed unable to move, much less flap their wings with force enough to lift themselves off the ground.

The sight of the birds feeding on Stirrup beef sent a wild anger coursing through Neil. He drew his gun, cursing, and was drawing a bead on one huge bald-headed king vulture when a voice spoke behind him.

"So now you know," the voice said.

Neil's body went rigid, and he came around in a slow pivot to look at the man who had spoken. It was Bat Gardner. He had one of his three friends from up north with him. They had stepped out, apparently, from a narrow niche between a pair of slablike rocks that jutted up some yards back from the cliff's edge.

They must have seen him coming, Neil realized bitterly. They'd assumed his curiosity would draw him over here for a look at what had attracted the buzzards, and they had lain in wait for him, laid this ambush for him.

Both of their guns were drawn, pointed at him, and they stood far enough apart so that he could concentrate his attention on only one of them at a time. Neil let his gun slip down into the holster, and gave a fatalistic shrug and smiled, putting the best face he could on this situation.

He was thinking of his cattle, dozens of them, cold-bloodedly butchered, as he said to Bat Gardner, "I never would've guessed you'd be such a bad loser."

'So now you know," Bat said again, "and now you're dead. We'll see what kind of a loser you are."

Neil stood rooted, helpless, hating himself for the carelessness that had let him blunder into this situation. But how was he to have guessed that he would find his beef run callously over a cliff to their destruction, that Bat Gardner's wounded vanity could drive him to such a brutal device by way of retaliation for a fancied wrong?

Neil studied the small man, then said tightly, "If you're going to shoot me, go ahead. Pull that trigger."

Bat's smile was cruel, without pity. "Just to show you what a big-hearted fellow I am, I'll give you your choice."

"What choice?"

"You can stand there and take a slug in the stomach," Bat said, "or you can take a jump." Again the little man grinned. "I never seen a man take a two-hundred-foot jump off a cliff. It might be worth seeing."

Neil stared at the man. Once, in a saloon up north, he had watched Bat Gardner play at the game of cat-and-mouse with a man who had inadvertently jostled him while standing beside him at the bar. Bat had toyed with the poor devil until he had him crawling, literally begging for mercy, and Neil knew the little man's vanity had fed on the other man's crumbling self-respect. Neil straightened his shoulders, telling himself he must not cringe, must not give the man that satisfaction, no matter what happened.

"I'm not going to make it that easy for you, Bat," he said. "You're going to have to pull that trigger."

The little man's reaction was characteristic of him. "I think you'll jump," he said, and he pulled the trigger. The slug whistled past Neil's head, so close he could feel the air disturbed by it. Bat had already palm-cocked the gun. He was grinning. "I can come closer than that," he said calmly.

Neil's mind had been numbed till now, but suddenly it cleared, and he was remembering that when he looked over the cliff's edge at his dead cattle he had seen a gnarled, stunted tree clinging tenaciously to the cliff's sheer face.

It was only twenty feet down, and it had had a sturdy look to it, as he remembered. If a man's weight were to hit that tree correctly, it would probably cushion his fall, and support him.

Bat Gardner's gun crashed again. This time the slug ripped at the cloth of Neil's shirt. He stepped back, glancing down past the lip of the drop until he saw the tree seeming to beckon him down below there.

He gave as good an imitation as he could of a man plunging to certain death, and stepped backward into space.

For one horrified instant as he fell, he was afraid he'd misjudged the target and would plunge past it. Then he came down on the tree, straddling its skinny trunk, which bent like a bow under his weight.

He waited until it stopped jiggling up and down, then wedged himself securely into position astride it and drew his gun.

He was looking up toward the lip of the drop, pointing the gun in that direction, when the head poked out into view for an instant. It was not Bat Gardner's head, but that of his sidekick.

Neil shot without compunction, saw his bullet catch the man under the chin, snapping his head back. The man fell back out of sight, away from the cliff's edge. Neil knew he was dead. The slug would have passed through the brain and out the top of the skull.

So now, he thought, he had only Bat to contend with. Holding his breath, he swung his glance along the rim up there above him. He was expecting Bat to show himself for the moment it would take to snap a shot at him, but time raveled on with no overture from Bat.

Bat Gardner, Neil reminded himself, was no fool. The little man had an animal cunning, enough to realize that he had all the advantage in this situation. He had mobility, whereas Neil was pinned helplessly to the face of the cliff, making a beautiful target.

He'll work his way into position for a shot at me, Neil thought angrily. It was only a question of time, as he saw it, and his glance ran up and down the face of the cliff, seeking some means of escape from this exposed position.

Some ten feet below him was a small ledge. It was no more than a couple of feet wide. A man attempting to drop onto it and not lose his balance would have to have glue on his boot soles. But it ran along the cliff's face for some distance, and at one point an overhang of rock above it would protect a man from attack.

Neil knew he had no choice but to try the mountain-goat stunt. Holstering his gun, he suspended himself from the tree, waited a moment until his body quit its gentle swinging, and let go.

He came down onto the ledge rockily, and one foot, hitting that unyielding stone only inches from the edge of the shelf, slid out into space.

Neil's reaction was reflective. He let his body go limp as an understuffed doll's, and came down on his hands, breaking the fall, and then hugged the ledge with all of his body.

It was all that saved him from plunging on down to the same fate that had been meted out to his cattle. He lay there panting a moment, then rose, hugging the rock wall, and worked himself along the face of the cliff.

The ledge ended abruptly under the overhang, where a slab of granite had crumbled off the cliff's face. If a man wanted to risk an eleven-foot jump to the other side of the gap, where the ledge continued its progress along the scarp, he could work his way clear over to one of the gulches, Neil saw.

Seeing that, he felt a swift exultation. He studied the jump for several minutes, eying the surface from which he must leap, estimating and re-estimating the distance. He finally decided he would need two steps to build up momentum, and he mapped them out as carefully as a general maps out a battle campaign involving the destiny of a nation.

He stepped back into position, adjusted the gun belt to a higher position around his waist so that it would not interfere with the free movement of his legs, drew one long breath, and took his pair of approach steps.

He was like a man running on ice, afraid to put much ginger into his movements for fear of losing his grip on the uncertain footing. When he got his left foot wedged over the lip of the drop, he put all the strength he had into a violent leap off that leg.

He was in the air then, looking down almost two hundred feet at the despoiled carcasses of his cattle. Time seemed to stand still for a moment, and then his reaching foot hooked itself over the edge of the ledge toward which he'd catapulted himself. He was falling short, he knew, and he let that leg bend at the knee, at the same time trying to hunch his upper body forward.

In that way he managed to convert a slight drop of his body's center of gravity into a little additional forward momentum. He was on the ledge then, landing in a scramble that took skin off both knees and an elbow.

He moved along the ledge until he reached the gully. A grim smile touched his mouth now, as he made his way cautiously up toward rimrock again, stalking Bat Gardner.

It took him ten minutes to work his way around the slablike rocks to the narrow niche from which Bat Gardner had emerged to get the drop on him.

He peered out narrowly and saw that Bat Gardner had been busy during the past fifteen minutes. The short man had rolled more than a dozen small boulders into place near the edge of the cliff, and now, as Neil watched, Bat Gardner moved deliberately along the line, kicking one heavy stone after another over the edge of the cliff.

Afterward, Bat Gardner lay prone beside his partner's dead body, shoved his hat back off his head, and peered carefully over the cliff.

Neil stepped out from the niche and said, "What do you see, Bat?"

He saw the tension strike through Bat Gardner's small body. The man's gun was in his hand, but he did not move, did not even turn his head for a look back over his shoulder.

"You wanted to see a man jump off a cliff, Bat," Neil told him. "That was your mistake. You saw what you wanted to see. Now you're going to pay the price of admission. Ease the gun into the holster and stand up."

"What's the idea?"

"The idea is that I've got a gun trained on the back of your head and I'm itching to pull this trigger."

Bat Gardner holstered his gun, stood up, automatically lifting his hands, and turned slowly to face Neil. A sullen puzzlement was in his eyes. It was plain he could not understand how a man could step off a two-hundred-foot cliff and then show up behind it fifteen minutes later.

"I ain't going to jump," he said, "if that's what you mean by the price of admission."

"No," Neil said, "you won't jump. But you'll fall." His gun was leveled on Bat as he spoke, but now he deliberately dropped it into the holster.

Bat Gardner looked at him as if he couldn't fathom such folly. A wicked pleasure leaped into the little man's eyes, and he whipped his hand down at his gun.

Neil had expected the man to strike without warning. His own draw seemed synchronized with that of the professional gunman, but he got his shot off a fraction of a second before the other man's gun crashed.

He felt the whistling breath of Bat Gardner's slug as it zipped by him. His own slug, because he had shot in such haste, took the small man in the shoulder, twisting him, driving him back.

For one moment Bat Gardner hung poised over the edge of the same cliff he'd forced Neil over at gunpoint. Panic twisted the man's ferret face as she swayed backward. He was screaming as he dropped out of sight, and Neil could hear that blood-curdling sound for several seconds.

It broke off with an abruptness that made Neil's body jerk in an involuntary reaction. He walked to the rim and peered down for some seconds at Bat Gardner's broken body, which had impaled itself on a needle-like stone.

A fluttery sensation touched him at the stomach, and all he wanted was to be away from here, quickly.

He turned away from the rimrock toward a little patch of grass where the gray horse was unconcernedly grazing.

Chapter Fourteen

A HALF A MILE from Frank Buckmaster's Broken Bit buildings, Peyt English reined in on his sorrel horse and sat staring down at the ground in bitter indecision.

All week he had listened to the bawling of thirsty cattle, and had told himself he'd be damned if he'd go crawling to Neil Ashton for water. He had tried to convince himself it would rain in time to save his herd.

The hoped-for rain had not come. This Friday morning, awakening to another cloudless day, he had made up his mind to do something. His pride still wouldn't let him approach Neil Ashton for a favor, but there was no reason, he felt, that Frank Buckmaster shouldn't give him a neighborly leg up.

The thought cheered him now as he trotted on toward Frank's buildings. Broken Bit, Peyt decided, had been a bachelor outfit too long. There wasn't a blade of grass on the place, and there were no flowers. A few spidery shrubs, which couldn't have been watered since the start of dry weather, were scattered about helter-skelter. The barns and corrals had a well-kept appearance, but there was no friendliness, no warmth to these buildings. Come to think of it, Peyt thought, there was no warmth to Frank, either.

Peyt's horse nickered, entering the yeard, and made for the trough. Peyt saw a battered tin cup hanging down from the pump on a makeshift wire hook. He climbed down and helped himself to a drink while his horse slopped up trough water.

The pump handle squealed as Peyt worked it, and that sound brought Frank around the corner of the barn. He lifted a hand to Peyt and came sauntering across the yard. He had his hired gunman, Johnny Winema, with him.

At sight of the half-breed, Peyt felt his face stiffen. He nodded a greeting to Frank, but ignored the half-breed.

He had no intention of exchanging pleasantries with a killer.

"Kind of off your usual beat, aren't you, Peyt?" Frank asked. "What's on your mind?"

Peyt directed a pointed glance at Winema and Frank waved Winema back toward the barn. The breed went over and sat in the dusty bed of a wagon, his legs dangling down against the dropped end gate. He took out makings and started to make himself a cigarette, eying Peyt with a faint, frowning anger.

"Let's have it," Frank said, and Peyt took the plunge then.

"I need help, Frank. My herd's going crazy for water. I noticed riding in here that most of your tanks are pretty full yet, and coming across the bridge just now I saw that your creek's not dry either. I was wondering if you could bail my herd out till we get a rain."

Frank was working the pump handle up and down idly, frowning as he listened.

"Your mistake," he said, "was in buyin' Heber out to being with. That's good grass down there on the Sunk, but water was always a problem for Heber. There's no show for you to make anything of that ranch, Peyt."

Peyt frowned. "What I'm interested in right now, Frank, is saving my herd. Can you help me?"

Frank was still working the pump handle up and down. Water spurted from the pump suddenly. Frank took the tin cup down from the wire hook and filled it. He drank a couple of mouthfuls and let the rest of the water dribble down into the trough, and then replaced the cup on the hook, something maddeningly deliberate in all these movements.

"I've got some water I could spare you right now," he admitted. "But I've seen too many of these droughts hit this country. There's never any way of predicting when it's going to break, and—"

"I'm not here asking for charity, Frank," Peyt said. "I'd pay you for the use of your water."

"That's not the point," Frank said, his mouth thinning.
"What is?"

"A week or so from now, if I water your herd for you like you're suggesting, my own herd could be in serious trouble." Frank glanced up slyly. "Why don't you go to Neil Ashton?"

Peyt explained what kept him from doing that, and Frank nodded. It was obvious that he approved of the position Peyt had taken with regard to accepting favors from Neil Ashton.

"Kind of puts you back of the eight ball, doesn't it?" Frank murmured, and he was silent a moment. "Might be one way I could help you."

"What's that?"

Frank paused, and then he looked up. "I'll be honest with you, Peyt. I would've liked to buy Heber out, but he sold out to you before I had any notion he was hunting a buyer. I could use that grass down there for a winter range, when water's no problem. If you'd be interested in selling—"

"I wouldn't," Peyt said in a clipped tone, and Frank gave a bland lift of his enormous shoulders.

"It'd be one way to keep that herd of yours from dyin' of thirst. Sell out to me and my crew'll have those cows up here and watered in a matter of hours."

Peyt scowled. "What would you give me for my holdings down there on the Sunk, Frank?"

Frank named a figure. It was less than half what Peyt had given Heber for the outfit. Peyt stared at the big man.

"You think I'm that crazy, Frank?" he asked thickly.

"That's my offer," Frank said, and he looked at Peyt, smiling. "You'd better take it. This drought's not going to break for a week or so yet. You stand to lose money either way. If you sell out to me, you won't have a couple thousand dead steers on your conscience."

"If you'd make me a decent price—"

"What's a decent price when two businessmen are sparrin' for an advantage?" Frank shrugged. "I'm offerin' what I think you'll accept."

Frank wore an expression of smug confidence. It seemed to say, "I've got you over a barrel, my friend," and Peyt stood there, feeling the lift of his temper.

107

He's glad my herd's hard up for water, Peyt thought, and he was struck by the contrast between Frank's reaction to the plight of the cattle and Neil Ashton's reaction.

Peyt English was beginning to see now what an idiot he had been to refuse Neil Ashton's generous offer to let him share Stirrup's lake water.

There was no other man to whom he could turn, Peyt knew. All the other outfits up here on the Bench would be skimping along on what little water they had, in no position to water another outfit's cattle.

Peyt knew he was going to have to eat crow and accept Neil Ashton's help, if it was still available to him. He faced up to the prospect without relish.

He glanced up at Frank.

"Thanks, Frank," he said. "Thanks for nothing."

Frank grinned at him, as if to say, "You'll be back, when you've thought about it."

Peyt walked to his horse, climbed up stiffly, and wheeled the animal out of the yard.

He rode from Frank's place across country toward Stirrup. The air was dry and thin, so that you could see for miles. As he came slanting in toward the Stirrup buildings, he saw a lone rider crossing a sagebrush flat north of him.

The rider was following the dim, seldom used trail that knifed down into the Bench from the Goshen Hole country. Watching the horseman as he came nearer, Peyt recognized Neil Ashton. He urged his sorrel horse across the flat in order to intercept Ashton.

Apologizing to any man never came easily for Peyt. But Neil Ashton grinned at him as they came together. Apparently he was no man to hold a grudge. Peyt said what he had to say, and was assured that Stirrup water was still available to his cattle. He thanked Ashton profusely.

"I just came from Broken Bit," Peyt said, and he described Frank's reaction to his request for water. Neil Ashton's face was thoughtful, then grim as he listened.

"I guess that does it," Neil said. "Frank has finally tipped his hand."

Peyt frowned. "I'm afraid I don't follow you, Ashton," he murmured.

"Frank's got the second most dependable water supply on the Bench," Neil said quietly. "I've got the best, because my lake is literally droughtproof. Frank's not afraid that I'll steal his cattle. His real reason for wanting me out of the country is so he can get hold of Stirrup. Don't you see why?"

"You mean he wants a corner on all the dependable water around here?" Peyt asked.

Neil nodded. "If Frank owned Stirrup, he'd have Le Bon and Llewellyn and all the rest of these ranchers around here over the same barrel he thought he had you over, when he made you that dirt-cheap offer for your outfit. There's never been any limit to Frank's ambition. He's always had it in his mind that he'd own the Bench someday. It's easy to see how he figures to do it, once he's got hold of Stirrup water."

There was inescapable logic, Peyt thought, in what Neil Ashton had said. If he had the power, Frank would force his neighbors off this range without a trace of compunction. Yes, and be within his legal rights, too. After all, there is no law that says a man must share what he has.

Le Bon and Llewellyn, all these Bench ranchers, would be forced, one by one, to capitulate and sell out to Frank if Frank owned all the dependable water. They'd knuckle down, Peyt knew, rather than see their herds suffer.

"Why don't you ask some of these other outfits for help, Ashton?" Peyt asked.

"I will," Neil said, "when I'm convinced there's no other answer. Not until then, though. Still seems to me there ought to be some way to narrow this fight down to myself and Frank. As I see it, Frank's trying to railroad me off my ranch and out of this country. It's more or less up to me to prove he can't get away with that."

"You're oversimplifying the situation," Peyt said. "All of us up here on the Bench have a stake in this fight. The future of the whole range depends on your sticking it out against Frank."

"I'd rather keep the fighting localized for a while yet,"

Neil said. "It may keep a few heads from being broken."

Peyt's eyes went wide with surprise. This was the man who'd been described to him in town as a thief and a killer. And he had accepted that estimate of the man without question!

He was beginning to appreciate, now, the enormity of the thing he had done in keeping quiet about the killing he had witnessed from the hilltop north of town. In a jealous attempt to injure Neil Ashton he had wronged this whole range.

Eying Ashton, he thought, Why don't I tell him I saw Winema kill the Kid and make things right with him? Until I do I'll never have any peace of mind.

Peyt opened his mouth, intending to speak, but some power stronger than the desire to make amends hobbled his tongue. Awkwardness overcame him. He felt the blood running up his neck into his cheeks. Without quite realizing what he did, he put out his hand.

It pleased him that his hand was accepted, without hesitation, and shaken warmly. He thanked Ashton again for his generosity, and touched spurs to the sorrel.

It occurred to him as he swung along the trail in the direction of his own distant headquarters that Neil Ashton, the man he had patronized and looked down his nose at, was in many ways a bigger man than he was.

These thoughts made him uncomfortable. He was only superficially aware of the trail unwinding beneath his horse's clip-clopping hoofs, of the animal's rhythmic, unceasing motion.

He was hardly prepared, as he rounded a granite outcrop that shouldered up out of flat prairie, to find Johnny Winema sitting his horse in the trail, waiting for him.

There was something unnerving in this unexpected encounter with the man he had nearly informed upon to Neil Ashton. Peyt nodded distractedly at the breed, and started to swing past him.

Winema jerked his mount broadside, blocking the trail, and Peyt blurted at him, "What's the idea?"

Winema grinned. "What was that between you and Neil Ashton?"

110

"Have you been following me, fellow?" Peyt glowered.

"Sure. On Frank's orders. Frank had an idea you might head for Stirrup and Neil Ashton." The breed's eyes took on a hard glitter. "You better learn to stay in the right stall, friend."

"I'll thank you to get out of my way," Peyt said stiffly.

Winema shook his head. "Frank wants you."

"Now see here—"

"My orders," Winema said, "was if you rode to Stirrup or in any way contacted Neil Ashton to bring you back, that's all. Come on."

Peyt winced, considering the prospect of another talk with Frank. Last week in Piperock Frank had warned him to stay on the right side of this quarrel. Peyt could imagine how Frank would react to the knowledge that he'd decided to accept help from Ashton. Frank's temper was notorious. The thought of it gave Peyt courage to say, "If Frank wants to see me he can see me at my place. Or in town."

Winema snickered and gave Peyt a look almost of pity. "Frank don't operate that way."

There was something beneath the surface here that Peyt didn't like. His rising fear erupted in a display of false anger. "I don't give a damn how Frank operates. That's how it's going to be, fellow."

Winema looked at him, not at all impressed by the outburst. "You can tell it to Frank when we get to Broken Bit. I'm only followin' his orders. Now get moving."

Peyt sat there like a stubborn child refusing a parental order. Ten seconds went by. Winema's horse, tired of standing, champed at the ground with one dainty forefoot.

The half-breed yanked at his reins, mouth-whipping the animal. Peyt knew that Winema was near the end of his patience, that the meanness in the man was about to surface.

He was caught now, he saw, in a web of his own spinning, for it came to him that this wouldn't be happening to him if he'd made the right decision that night he'd seen Winema commit murder. He felt a sour regret for his failure

111

to make a clean breast of things a few minutes ago, when he'd been with Neil Ashton.

On an impulse he reached inside his coat, as if to pull out a cigarette or some equally innocent object, and pulled the compact little derringer from the well-camouflaged shoulder holster.

He pointed the weapon at the half-breed. Winema's eyes took on a pinched look of surprise. He carefully lifted his grimy brown hands. He made no gesture at his own hip-holstered six-gun. He stared with an odd mixture of contempt and respect at the tiny pistol Peyt held. His eyes came up to Peyt's.

"Anyone ever tell you it ain't smart to pull a gun unless you're fixing to use it?"

The man's attitude galled Peyt. Winema seemed to regard the derringer as a woman's weapon, and that, more than anything else, oddly enough, influenced Peyt toward a drastic decision. He would take this insolent fellow into Piperock, hand him over to Roy Millership, and prefer charges against him for the Kid's murder.

"Don't think I'm not willing to use it," Peyt said. He saw Winema's fleeting smile, and went on angrily, "Drop your left hand to your belt. Loosen the buckle and let the belt fall. Keep your other hand nice and high. And don't smile. I'm not fooling."

To prove that he wasn't, he put a little pressure against the trigger. Winema shrugged and dropped one bronzed hand to the clasp of the cartridge belt, as directed.

Peyt watched the man, wary of him, knowing he could not afford to relax until Winema's belt and gun had dropped to the ground. Having the drop on this man who was half civilized, half savage, was like holding a rattlesnake under one's foot. There was always the chance that he'd wriggle free and maneuver into striking position.

Winema's belt had a glossy, new look about it. The unworked leather was stiff. The half-breed was having trouble unfastening the buckle.

As he worked with one hand, awkward at the task, his horse restlessly sidled toward Peyt's horse. It occurred to Peyt that the breed might have kneed his animal on its off side, causing that shift of position, but he decided it was a natural restlessness on the part of the horse, and thought no more of it. His attention was focused on Winema's hand, working at the stiff buckle, and this was where he made his mistake.

Winema, shrewdly gauging the depth of Peyt's distraction, eased his near foot from the stirrup. He kicked up and out smartly.

The toe of the breed's boot caught Peyt just at the wrist, paralyzing his gun hand. The derringer flew from his nerveless fingers and landed in grass, the cushioned impact failing to discharge the weapon.

Winema's hand streaked to the gun at his hip. It flicked through Peyt's panicked mind that the man would shoot him down now, and he brought up his hands in a gesture that was half supplication, half an instinctive but foolish attempt to fend off the man's bullet.

He tried to choke out a plea for mercy. The words curdled in his throat as he watched Winema flip his gun end over end and swing it down like a bludgeon. The thought flicked through Peyt's mind that a shot now could be embarrassing to Winema, could bring Neil Ashton running.

That thought completed itself, and then the heavy stock of Winema's gun struck, and Peyt's brain exploded.

Chapter Fifteen

FRANK BUCKMASTER was out in the patio, taking the air, when Johnny Winema trotted into the ranchyard. One glance at the gunman's set expression was enough to rouse Frank to a quick concern. He had seen that look of sullen guilt on Winema's face once before.

Some of Frank's riders, having knocked off work for the day, lounged on the bunkhouse steps, smoking and idly conversing. They looked up, watching Winema as he climbed down and dropped his reins over the hitch rack in front of the house. Their eyes followed Johnny as he crossed the patio flagstones to where Frank stood by the office door.

113

Frank took the breed by the elbow and led him inside, away from the too-curious eyes. Propping himself against a sturdy oak table piled high with account books and ledgers, Frank regarded the gunman.

"Let's have it," he grunted.

His mouth went taut as he heard Winema's account of what had happened. Although he had known something must have gone wrong, Frank was hardly prepared to accept without blinking the information that Peyt English was dead, his skull crushed in by a blow from Winema's six-gun.

Frank's first reaction was one of shocked disbelief. This was followed, in turn, by acceptance and a wild anger. He lifted a fisted hand at the half-breed, and then checked the impulse to hit him. This was no time for temper, an inner voice warned him coolly.

"Relax," Frank said to Winema, who was eying him the way a man eyes a horse with a reputation for meanness.

"Relaxing ain't easy right now, Frank. If you ask me, this is big trouble."

Frank hardly heard him. His mind was busy. It seemed unlikely that Peyt English could have had sense enough to keep quiet about Frank's attempt to buy him out. No, Frank thought, Peyt probably did some whining to Neil Ashton about the way I refused him use of my water.

Frank knew a moment's regret for the impulse that had prompted him to make Peyt that offer. Simple greed, and an overwhelming desire to try out his plan for conquest of the Bench beforehand, using Peyt as a test case, had betrayed him into making a premature move, and he swore at his own folly.

Winema was saying, "How are you fixed for ready cash, Frank?"

Frank's guard went up at the mention of money. He said, "I'm not," and then, in a more reasonable tone of voice, he asked, "Why?"

"I can be across the state line before dark," Winema pointed out, "and a hundred miles from here before sun-up tomorrow."

Frank looked at the man, frowning, not seeing him really.

It was hard to pull his thoughts together. Neil Ashton was nobody's fool. It wouldn't take him long, once he knew Frank had tried to buy Peyt English out rather than water his thirsty cattle, to figure out what Frank's game was.

Frank swore, Peyt English's death, and the fact that Winema had killed him, were trial enough for any man's temper. The realization that Neil must be aware of his plan of conquest, and could use the knowledge of it against him, worried Frank more, though.

"Is there any chance Neil Ashton saw you with English?" he asked.

Winema finger-combed his greasy hair nervously. "He couldn't have. I laid in wait for English back of a big stone outcrop." The half-breed was watching Frank's expression. Something almost wistful came into the breed's manner as he said, "All I'd need for getaway money is a couple hundred."

Frank scowled, reminded of a dog begging. "Maybe there won't be any need for you to run, Johnny."

Winema looked up, his eyes narrowing, uneasiness in them. "I don't know what you've got in your mind, Frank," he said. "Personally, I ain't in no mood to take chances."

Frank's jaws clicked shut as he regarded the half-breed. "This makes the second time in less than a month that my back's been shoved to the wall, thanks to your bulgling. I think you'll take a chance now if I tell you to, Johnny."

Winema looked at the floor, frowning.

Frank said, "It's my instinct at a time like this to hit out. Neil Ashton's probably seen the light, and we got to keep him off balance."

"How?"

"Tell the boys to saddle up," Frank said, with a jerk of his head toward the bunkhouse. "We're riding to town."

Winema looked perplexedly at him. "I don't—"

"On our way in," Frank said, "we'll just happen to discover Peyt English's body there where you left it beside the trail. Act surprised, Johnny, when we find him."

The breed acted even more mystified now. "What for?"

"When you've bashed in a man's head with the butt end

115

of a six-gun," Frank said with heavy sarcasm, "it's a good idea to keep people from knowing you did it. Some of those boys out there in the bunkhouse may guess at the truth when we find Peyt's body. We'll keep them guessing."

"What's the play, Frank?"

Frank smiled. "When we get into town with Peyt's body," he said, "keep your eyes open, Johnny. You may learn something."

It was all the satisfaction he gave the half-breed.

By the time Frank and his Broken Bit riders pulled up to a hock-rattling halt in front of the Piperock Hotel's peeling hitch rack, the first long shadows of early evening lay over the street.

News that a dead man was being brought into Piperock had preceded Frank and his men into town. They were quickly surrounded by a crowd of jostling, clamoring curiosity seekers.

Frank saw one small boy, who could not have been more than six or seven years old, staring with morbid eyes at Peyt English's body, which hung limply over a horse's back.

Frank's glance seldom missed much that was worth seeing, and now he saw Lena Le Bon peering out through the hotel door. He wondered disinterestedly what sort of errand had brought the girl into town and kept her here past the dinner hour. Then he forgot her as the crowd began to pummel him and his men with questions.

On the way into town Frank had told his men that he would do any talking that became necessary. He didn't propose to do any just yet. He sat his huge roan, blandly ignoring the demands for information. He waited for five full minutes, with unruffled composure, until Marshal Roy Millership put in his appearance.

A heavy silence fell over the street as Millership came along the plank walk, his heel taps resounding, and halted before Frank and his riders. The tension among the onlookers was an almost tangible thing. You could smell it, Frank thought, and he grinned smugly, for he had purposely set the stage this way. Anything he said now in response to Millership's inevitable questions, he knew, would be listened to by the crowd with rapt attention.

116

Roy Millership hitched up his pants on his skinny hips, and nodded at Peyt English's body draped over the horse. "What about this, Frank?"

Frank cleared his throat. "You know almost as much about it as I do. Peyt come callin' on me this afternoon at Broken Bit. Said his herd was in a bad way for water, and wondered if I could spare his critters a drink to carry them over till the next rain. I told him Neil Ashton was the man really fixed right for water around here. I said if Ashton refused to help him, he could come back to me and I'd do what I could for him."

Frank paused for breath, and continued: "He rode out, actin' kind of displeased about it. So then later on, when me and the boys was ridin' down here for our usual weekend blowoff, we found him lyin' in the trail a mile or so out of Stirrup. His head's been bashed in, Roy." Anger ruffled Frank's voice as he said, "I don't guess there's much question who did it."

Millership chose to play stupid. "Who, Frank?"

Frank was aware that the crowd had become absolutely still, waiting for him to answer the marshal. He told himself to walk softly now, not lay it on.

"I've told you what I know, Roy," he said. "Draw your own conclusions."

"Are you saying Neil Ashton killed Peyt English?"

Frank met the man's stare, and shrugged for the benefit of those who were watching. One of Peyt English's crewmen stepped forward reluctantly, and spoke to the marshal.

"There's somethin' you'd better know, Roy," said the puncher. "It's my understandin' that the boss and Neil Ashton had a kind of ruckus early this week."

"What about?" Millership acted as though he hated to ask the question.

"The way I understand it, Ashton came over to ask the boss if he could make use of that Stirrup water. The boss turned him down, too proud to accept help from him, I reckon. I hear it pretty near come to a shooting."

The crowd murmured at that, and Frank grinned without moving his mouth. This was luck he hadn't hoped for.

"Add up any better now, does it?" he asked the marshal.

Millership scowled. He kept shaking his head, as though he couldn't bring himself to believe Neil capable of butchering a man as Peyt English had been butchered. The crowd, Frank saw, was not nearly so reluctant to condemn Neil, and he was careful not to smile.

"Hell, Roy," he said, playing the role of a patient, reasonable man for the moment, "who else had any reason to kill him? He was a well-liked man around here."

Roy Millership didn't say anything to that. Frank pressed his advantage: "Roy, there's been bad blood between those two since Neil's first day back here in Piperock. I've got a hunch Ruth Orr could give us more information about that, if she had a mind to."

"Until you've got something definite to indicate that Neil might have done this," Millership snapped, "let's leave Ruth Orr's name out of it, Frank."

There were enough gallant fools in this crowd, Frank saw, to sway the sentiment of the whole bunch toward the marshal's viewpoint. It angered Frank, and he let temper have its way with him now, knowing shrewdly that one man's righteous wrath can have an electrifying effect on a crowd.

"That's a dead man lying over that horse, Roy. I had a lot of regard for Peyt English, and I'm in no state of mind to mince words. They tell me here in town that Neil and Peyt, came to blows Neil's first day back. Seems to me, you bein' town marshal, you might've taken the trouble to look into that."

"I did," Millership said. "There wasn't much to it. It happened in the Crescent. They had a scuffle."

"Hold on, Roy," an onlooker said. "I heard about that. As I understand it, English tried for his gun and Ashton damn near broke his jaw for him. That ain't what I'd call a scuffle."

Frank grinned.

Millership said, "You haven't proved anything, Frank."

"You tell me who killed him," Frank said. "Who else had any reason to kill him?"

118

Millership shook his head, bafflement in his eyes. Frank waited, letting the marshal's uncertainty register with the crowd. It seemed a good note to end on, and disregarding Roy Millership now, Frank walked his horse down the street. His men followed. Minutes later, in the back room at Happy Jack's, Frank lifted a glass of his favorite whisky in a victory salute to Johnny Winema.

"Learn anything?" Frank asked.

"I ain't so sure you sold a bill of goods to the marshal."

"I wasn't trying to sell Roy. I was selling this town."

"I don't know, Frank. I ain't so sure about this."

"Isn't there any gambling blood in you?" Frank grumbled.

"Not where my neck's concerned."

"You'll gamble," Frank said, "whether you want to or not. You've put me out on thin ice. You'll stick around until I'm safely off it." Frank pointed at Winema's glass on the table. "Drink up, and quit whining."

Chapter Sixteen

NEIL TETHERED his horse in a clump of sagebrush south of the railroad tracks and picked his way cautiously into town on foot by moonlight. He cut across a weed-grown vacant lot, approaching Ruth's house from the rear, and rapped lightly on the door.

He could hear Ruth's graceful, feather-light footfalls as she came from the front of the house toward the kitchen, and then across the kitchen to the door. Her muffled voice reached him through the panel.

"Who is it?"

Neil identified himself. Ruth slid the bolt and let him in. She went across the kitchen and pulled down both blinds before she struck a match to the lamp hanging down from the ceiling.

As she dropped her spent match into the coal scuttle, Neil looked closely at her, and saw that she had been crying.

119

"I guess you've heard about Peyt," Ruth said in a lifeless low voice, and Neil nodded.

Lena Le Bon, who apparently was no longer angry with him for having turned down her offer of partnership with her father, had sent a 66-puncher to Stirrup with the news of what had happened to Peyt, and of what Frank was up to here in Piperock.

Neil had sent Bill Marion down to Peyt's headquarters on the Sunk to tell Peyt's crew what had happened, and to tell them that Stirrup water was available to their thirst-crazed cattle.

That had been hours ago, and Neil still couldn't quite accept the fact that Peyt English was dead. His own luck, he knew dismally, had run out at the same time that Peyt English's had.

"I understand I'm supposed to have killed him, Ruth," he said. "I didn't want any question in your mind about that. That's why I'm here."

The blue eyes came up, and she attempted a smile, which fluttered and died. "I knew you couldn't have killed him."

Neil told her about his talk with Pyet, told her what Peyt had told him about Frank's attempt to buy him out. Ruth listened with her head down, a sort of dull misery touching her face.

Neil wondered if, in her grief, she would see that what Frank had tried to put over on Peyt was only a sample. For a while this afternoon, after his talk with Peyt, Neil had seen victory within his grasp, certain. It had seemed to him that Frank, in attempting to buy Peyt out before acquiring Stirrup's water, had committed a classic blunder.

When Neil's ranching neighbors learned of it they could hardly fail to realize their danger. Neil would have their help whether he liked it or not, he had told himself several hours ago. Now, however, he saw only trouble ahead of him.

Although the case Frank had built against him here in town was circumstantial, Frank had marshaled the evidence against him with a cruel cunning. A jury could hardly help being prejudiced against a man with Neil's background.

Frank would make all he could of the fact that Neil had killed a man up north. Neil felt a bleak admiration for Frank, who never overlooked a chance to hit out at an opponent.

Ruth slumped into a chair and dropped her arms onto the kitchen table. Shock had etched deep lines into her face. "You've got to get out of town, Neil."

"Why have I?"

"Roy Millership was in to see me earlier tonight. He told me that Frank's been making the rounds of the saloons, putting in a word here and there, wherever it's likely to do you the most damage."

"Where's Johnny Winema?"

Ruth's eyes darkened as she looked at him. "Why?"

He wasn't sure, himself, why he'd asked the question. There was his belief, which time had strengthened, that Winema had killed the Kid, and a feeling now that Winema might be responsible for the death of Peyt English.

"Just wondered," he murmured.

"He's here in town with Frank," Ruth said. She folded her smooth hands on the table. "Roy has sent to Cheyenne for Sheriff Hendy. Roy's worried, Neil. He's hoping you'll stay out of sight until the sheriff gets here. He says he wouldn't put it past Frank to try to whip up a lynch party for you."

Neil grinned, but Ruth's eyes remained starkly sober, as though she could see nothing but trouble in this situation. Her concern for his safety warmed him. He fought off an impulse to reach down for one of Ruth's hands. Somehow the man who had died today was in this room, coming between him and Ruth. He could not fight that, he realized.

"I'm sorry about Peyt, Ruth," he said simply. "I never got to know him, but if you were willing to marry him he must have been quite a fellow."

She gave a tired little lift of her shoulders. "I'd changed my mind about marrying him," she said quietly. "It wouldn't have worked. He wanted to put a ring on my finger the night the Kid was killed. I wouldn't let him. He acted pretty put out, but I think when he'd had time to

121

think about it he must have realized that neither of us would have been happy."

Neil had stopped breathing, and his throat had gone dry.

"Ruth," he said, "this fight with Frank has got to end sometime. I know it looks pretty black now, but there's no telling what might happen. When this fight's over, if I should happen to win, I'd have something substantial to offer. I—"

"Please," Ruth said softly, "not now," and Neil nodded understandingly, and changed the subject.

He excused himself presently, and let himself out into the night-shrouded yard. He couldn't get it out of his mind that Ruth had refuesd to wear Peyt English's ring. He had no rival, then, in the memory of the dead man, and he found that realization exciting.

"You're not careful, Ashton."

The voice hit out at him from behind one of Ruth's lilac bushes. It was the voice of Wes Benedict, the Broken Bit puncher who had spied on him as he made his prodigal's return to this country. As he recognized Benedict's voice, Neil felt paralysis work its way up through his body.

Instead of woolgathering over what Ruth had said, romantic as any schoolboy, he should have been considering the risk that he ran in being here. He should have been watching these shadows.

Wes Benedict stepped out, gun in hand, from behind the lilac bush. Moonlight touched the man's face. Neil saw that he was grinning.

"I watched you go in," Wes said, "but I wasn't sure it was you. So I waited."

Neil's glance dropped to the leveled gun. He lifted his hands, frowning faintly. "You don't want me, Wes."

"Frank does." Wes Benedict's voice held no rancor, only a weary puzzlement as he said, "What're you doin' here in town after killing Peyt English? You want to stretch a rope, do you?"

Neil shook his head. "I didn't kill him. Frank knows it. And I think you know it."

Wes Benedict snorted. "Whose leg are you pulling? The whole town knows you did it."

"The whole town knows wrong."

Benedict's shoulders jerked with impatience. He had allowed the muzzle of his gun to drop a trifle. He brought it up to line on Neil's chest, and jerked his head toward the center of town.

"Walk," he said.

Neil did not move. From somewhere uptown came the muted tinkling of a piano, a man's shouted laugh, and the answering laugh of a woman. The saloons along Main Street, it seemed to Neil, were putting out more than their usual racket. He wondered if Frank, who ordinarily was close with his money, could be setting up drinks for the town's riffraff.

It was the time-honored way of lining up recruits for a lynch party. It was an angle that Frank would not overlook. Neil knew suddenly, with the impact of solid conviction, that it would not do to let Benedict take him to Frank. He'd stretch a hang rope before morning.

"Walk, I said, Ashton!"

There was a rasping anger in Wes Benedict's voice, but it was anger, Neil felt, that had no bottom to it. This tall, bandy-legged puncher gave an impression of toughness; he seemed to fit in with Frank's hardcase crew. But Neil had a hunch that most of Wes Benedict's toughness lay on the surface.

Neil nodded at the gun leveled at him. "I don't think you'd shoot a man down in cold blood, Wes."

Benedict's eyes went thin. He took a step forward. "Try me," he suggested.

Neil hesitated, debating whether to face Frank in the role of a captive or to risk this man's temper. Deliberately he turned his back on the puncher, on the gun.

"Pull the trigger, Wes," he said over his shoulder, "if you're going to."

"Are you crazy?" the man snapped. "Turn around."

Neil didn't move. "It's going to have to be in the back," he said, and he added, "Any idea what happens to you, Wes, when you shoot a man in the back?"

"Damnit, I said turn around!"

"You hang," Neil said. "For murder."

He could hear Benedict drag in a quick breath. Neil stood there mentally ticking off seconds. When he got up to ten he started to walk away from the man with the gun, moving with slow, deliberate steps, angling toward the street, toward the railroad depot and freight yards.

"Ashton!"

Wes Benedict gritted it out. Neil's steps faltered. Halting, he heard the puncher take two plunging steps in pursuit. He knew intuitively that he had pushed the situation to the breaking point.

Neil shrugged and again raised his hands. He was turning to face Wes Benedict when the man's gun crashed and thrust out its flaming tongue at him.

That turn of his body as Benedict triggered was all that saved him from taking a bullet in the small of his back. As it was, the slug caught him in the shoulder, spinning him, knocking him off balance.

Staggering to one side, he barely managed to stay on his feet. Wes Benedict, seeing that he didn't fall, thumbed back the hammer of his gun and brought it up in panic.

Neil's reaction to the threat was instinctive. His hand snapped down and yanked the gun from the scabbard. He was cocking the weapon as he brought it up. He spanked out his shot without waste motion.

Benedict's body jerked like a string-dangling puppet's. He swayed an instant, a low wheezing breath sliding past his slack lips, and then he went to his knees.

He was like that for three seconds, oddly like a man praying, before he toppled, furrowing the dirt with his nose.

Behind Neil at an upstairs window one of Ruth's boarders called out in the peevish voice of a man whose sleep has been interrupted, "What's goin' on down there?"

From the center of town came the sound of a door thrown violently open, then slammed, and a pounding of booted feet on the planks of the boardwalk.

Neil heard men shouting to one another in the dark. He heard a voice say, somewhere up there on Main Street, "That shot came from down on Third Street. Who's supposed to be watchin' Miss Orr's house?"

124

Neil holstered his gun, from which a tendril of acrid smoke was rising, and ran across the lot adjoining Ruth's lot to the freight yard fence. Luckily the fence was not very high. He clambered over it, favoring his injured left side and collecting a splinter in transit.

He lay in a tangle of rank grass on the other side of the fence, his chest heaving from the slight exertion. Blood had started to work its way down his arm. Oddly, the pain hadn't set in yet. There was only a sort of dull ache in the shoulder.

The hunt was on now. He could hear men running down Third Street, calling out to one another. He heard a voice say, "Let's have a lantern over here, somebody. On the double," and he knew then they had located Wes Benedict's body.

Neil stood up gingerly, silently, so as not to betray his presence here behind the low fence, and picked his way across the dark freight yard. He'd gone only twenty yards when he heard Frank's voice, back there where he'd left the man on the ground.

"Here's blood," Frank was saying, and Neil paused by the gloomy bulk of a boxcar to listen.

"Wes must have winged him, boys," Frank said. "He's afoot and hurt bad, judgin' by the amount of blood he's left behind him. Some of you chase back uptown and round up every lantern you can lay your hands on."

"Hell, Frank," a voice said, "you ain't proposing to track him down by lamplight?"

"I'm declaring open season on him," Frank grated. "This time he's gone too damn far. I've got five hundred dollars for the man that puts a bullet into him."

Neil's lips compressed. Five hundred dollars. It was a small fortune, more than a year's pay for the average cowpuncher. There were men in Frank's crew who would slit their mothers' throats for less money than that.

They'll hunt me down, Neil thought. It will be like a game, like a treasure hunt for them.

He stumbled around a string of cattle cars on a siding. Blood had seeped all the way down his arm into his palm.

He closed his fingers experimentally on it, and a wicked pain struck him in the shoulder.

He almost blanked out. He could hear Frank's men shouting behind him. That sound put a terrible urgency into him as he left the freight yard and stumbled toward the clump of sagebrush where he'd left his horse.

He wondered dismally if he had strength enough to lift himself onto the animal's back.

Chapter Seventeen

HE DRAGGED into 66 around midnight, and by then he was flirting with unconsciousness, as badly done in as a man can be and remain in a saddle. A big, excitable mutt picked him up as he neared the Le Bon buildings.

Neil used up a precious driblet of energy cursing the brute, but the dog wouldn't be still. It yapped at him, and nipped at his horse's front feet. The gray broke gait in order to kick out at the dog. The lurching movement of the animal under him jarred Neil, and it felt for a moment as though someone had struck a long knife into his shoulder.

He clung miserably to the horn, nauseated, his world swimming, swirling crazily about him. He could feel himself pitching slowly forward and down, against the gray's neck. The coarse, bristly hair of the animal's mane rubbed against his cheek. The last thing he remembered was the strong smell of horse in his nostrils. . . .

"Neil, wake up." It was Lena's voice, nagging at him, persistent, cruel in its refusal to let him rest. "Wake up. You've got to. You've got to wake up now."

Neil opened his eyes. He was lying, fully dressed, on the counterpane of a sturdy four-poster bed. Lena was leaning over him, a sharp concern in her face. She seemed relieved, now that he'd awakened. She settled into a chair at the bedside, and Neil stared groggily at her. The gunshot wound in his shoulder, he saw, had been cleaned and bandaged.

"Who do I thank for the medical service?" he asked, flicking his eyes at the shoulder.

"One of the boys in our bunkhouse. Neil, I hated having to wake you up, but I had no choice. You've got to get away from here. In another hour it will be daylight."

Neil's eyes widened at her. "How long have I been out?" he asked, frowning.

"Almost five hours. Neil, I'm worried for you. One of our riders just rode in from town with the latest on what Frank is up to. Frank's split his crew into three posses, and they've orders to shoot you down on sight. They'll trail you here the minute the sun comes up and gives them enough light to follow sign by."

Neil knew she was right. He thought briefly of trying to make it up to Stirrup, but that was exactly where Frank would expect him to head for, and he knew if he rode that way he would probably ride into an ambush. He felt a gray animosity toward Frank, who had him on the run now and would play the old game of fox and hounds with him, showing him no mercy whatever.

He sat up experimentally on the bed. Pain stabbed at the injured shoulder, but he carefully refrained from wincing. For Lena's benefit, he even managed a crooked smile.

"Is my horse saddled?"

"In the yard," Lena said. "Waiting for you." She was watching him with a sharp, faintly proprietary look in her dark eyes. She pointed at his bandaged shoulder and asked bluntly, "How far do you think you'll get with that?"

Neil shook his head. "I don't know. I'd rather ride out than wait here for them, though."

"Neil, I've been thinking," Lena said, and the crisp way she spoke indicated that she had been giving a great deal of thought to what she was about to broach to him. "Why couldn't we ride as far as the railroad and try to flag down the westbound when it comes through this morning?"

There was a kind of apathy in Neil that dulled his responses. He tried to concentrate on what Lena was suggesting. "The engineer," he murmured wearily, "would never stop for us, Lena."

"I think he would," she said, and smiled a bit proudly, "for a pretty girl."

Neil looked thoughtfully at her. "He might, at that," he

admitted, and a swift hope ran joltingly through him. The westbound, he was thinking, came through this country at the first crack of sunrise. If they could get the train to stop somewhere between Piperock and Cheyenne and take him aboard . . . He broke off the chain of thought, shaking his head, scowling at the mental picture of himself on a train, a hunted man with a bullet hole through his shoulder, without friends, at the mercy of his fellow passengers, strangers.

"It's no good, Lena," he sighed. "It's no good at all, without money. I'd have to buy help, all the way, and—"

"There's nearly a thousand dollars in Dad's office," Lena said, and Neil, without thinking, looked at her and asked: "How do you know?"

"Dad's eyes have been acting up on him lately. I've been working the combination of the safe for him." She was looking straight at him, and there was something brittle, without feeling in her voice as she added, "Dad isn't here, Neil. He's off on another horse-buying junket."

Neil didn't say anything, he only looked at her, and Lena said, "Neil, it would work. We could be a hundred miles away before Frank and that crew of his even guessed what the play was."

"We?" Neil asked, lifting an eyebrow.

Lena still looked straight into his eyes. Her cheeks were flushed, not with embarrassment, but with excitement, he gathered. He was certain this girl had not lost her composure.

She said, "With a thousand dollars in our pocket we could ride all the way through to the end of the line, to San Francisco. We could put up at a hotel. I'd nurse you until your shoulder was better and—"

"Are you sure," Neil asked, "you know what you're suggesting?"

"I know exactly what I'm suggesting," Lena said, and her eyes touched his again, something bold in them. "I'm hoping you'll marry me, Neil, when we get to San Francisco."

He said, "You're not serious, Lena."

"I hope I'm never more so."

Neil said wonderingly, "You'd do that for me?"

"I'd do a lot more than that, Neil, to keep you from being shot by a posse."

"What about your dad?" Neil asked her.

"What about him?"

Neil frowned a little. "Don't you care?"

She shrugged her trim shoulders. There was something catlike, Neil thought, in the callous gesture. "Dad's life isn't in danger," she said. "Yours is. That's all I care about now, Neil."

She was offering him a way out, Neil thought. Not a way a man could be proud of, but the only way she could think of, and he supposed he ought to feel gratitude. Another man would probably jump at it, he thought, studying the perfect oval of this girl's face, the provocative curves of her young body, and he wondered why he was not tempted.

Lena, watching him, said, "Dad would hit the ceiling at first, Neil, but then he'd forgive us. He'd send us more money, if I wrote him for it. He'll never disown me, I know that."

He had the feeling of being baited, like a fat fish hovering about the hook, and he felt something within him coiling against her.

Lena said, "It's the only way you'll get out of this country alive. Frank won't rest now till he's made sure you're dead and out of his way, Neil. . . . And what if Dad is hurt a little? Dad's old. He's had his life. It's our turn to live now. Don't we have a right to be happy?"

"Can we be happy that way?" Neil asked.

Lena frowned at him. "What's bothering you?"

"Your dad," Neil said. "He's always shot square with me, Lena." He rubbed a hand over his eyes, then rose gingerly from the bed and walked to the door of this tiny bedroom.

He could hear Lena's chair scrape the floor as she rose quickly behind him. "What's got into you, Neil?" she snapped. "Where are you going?"

He turned with his hand on the doorknob, eying her with a smiling tolerance now. "I couldn't do that to Jules, Lena."

Her pretty chin sagged, and he saw the disbelief in the luminous black eyes. "Not even to save your life?"

"Not to save my life," Neil said.

Lena's little laugh had a peculiar, off-key resonance to it. "What's the matter with me?" she asked. "Something pretty horrible must be, when a man won't have me to save his life."

"Lena," he murmured, "you've got this all wrong." He had meant to say more, but he cut it off short, seeing the angry stain in her cheeks.

"Oh, get out. Get out!" she snapped, clenching both her small hands, and she stamped one foot at him.

"Thanks, anyway," Neil said, meaning it, and he turned away then. Going out, he left the door open, but a breath of air stirring through the house caught the door, and swung it closed. There was an odd finality in the sound it made as it clicked shut behind him.

He went out to the yard, where his gray horse stood waiting, and hauled himself painfully to the saddle. He rode out of 66 in that down-pressing darkness that precedes dawn by an hour, and by the time the sun was well up in the east he was easing himself down off the gray's back in Tietown.

Tietown wasn't really a town, only a little cluster of rotting, unpainted shacks marking the site of an abandoned lumber camp that had once produced ties for the railroad. It lay hidden, all but forgotten, in a crease of low wooded hills twelve miles west of Piperock.

Neil pulled the gray horse into a tangle of buckbrush at the edge of a clearing, tying the animal there, and then put his back to the bole of a tree, taking in these sagging buildings, the pungent odor of rotted wood crinkling his nostrils. Years ago, as a youngster rattling about the range without supervision, he had discovered this place, and had made it one of his favored haunts. It had not changed much.

On the way down here from Lena's place he had used every device he could think of to confuse a tracker. Now he picked out what looked like a soft spot in the grass and lay down, telling himself he could afford to relax for a while. He stared up at feathery clouds scudding across the blue sky, and tried to keep himself awake by thinking of Ruth. Exhaustion eventually won the uneven battle. His eyes closed and he slept.

He came awake with a high sun blazing on his face, knowing it wasn't the noon sun that had awakened him, knowing in some way he could not explain that he was in danger.

He sat up, all his senses alerted, and he heard it then, the faint click of a horse's shod hoof against the stone. The sound came from downslope, where this little crease in the hillside spilled out onto the sage flat.

Neil peered out from behind a cluster of boulders and saw Johnny Winema moving slowly and very deliberately up the slope toward him. The gunman was scanning the ground ahead of him, reining in on his horse occasionally, as a man does when reading sign.

He was less than a quarter-mile from Neil, and he came on up the slope with the boldness of a man who had no inkling that he had arrived within shooting distance of his quarry.

After all, Neil thought, that sign he's following is hours old.

The breed's presence here, alone, could be explained in only one way. Winema had cut his sign and trailed him down here alone because he wanted that five-hundred-dollar bounty Frank had offered, and had no intention of sharing it with his fellow crewmen.

A carbine in a crude scabbard was suspended from the breed's saddle horn. Neil had only his six-gun, and would be at a fatal disadvantage in any exchange of shots other than at short range.

He eyed his horse, concealed in the buckbrush, and knew it was only a question of time until the animal, scenting Winema's horse, would betray his presence here to the half-breed.

Neil realized he couldn't afford to let that happen. He hurried across the clearing toward a thick stand of piñons. Once under the evergreen cover, with a needle carpet to muffle his footfalls, he started down the grade at a long-striding run.

His ankle turned on a stone covered over by pine needles.

He fell heavily, and rolled up onto his feet. The bullet wound in his shoulder broke open, and he paused, feeling the blood ooze out under the dressing.

He moved downgrade more carefully after that. He swung over presently to the edge of the crease, and lay down behind a thick cluster of rabbit brush.

He could see Winema working his way deliberately up the grade. The breed was almost but not quite within range of Neil's pistol. He pulled his horse to a halt, and Neil frowned as he watched the man, for Winema wasn't studying the ground now.

The gunman sent a wary glance up the slope, and then glanced out quickly to either side of him.

That damned half-breed, Neil thought, has smelled something. He tucked his head down behind the rabbit brush as Winema's eyes shuttled toward him.

He had a decision to make now, and only an instant to make it. He could lie here in the hope that Winema would keep coming, or he could desert this place of hiding and charge the man in an attempt to get in close enough for an effective shot with his pistol.

He lifted his head slowly for another look at the half-breed. Winema's glance, by the worst luck imaginable, happened to be swinging at him in that instant. The man's eyes seemed to click into focus, widening at him.

The gunman's body had gone ramrod stiff, and Neil, realizing that circumstance had made the choice for him, didn't wait. He reared up from behind the rabbit brush and ran downhill toward the man, brandishing a cocked six-gun.

Winema stared at him in an unbelieving way, and then grinned. He started to take the carbine out of its sling. It was tightly wedged into the scabbard. During the few seconds he struggled with it, Neil covered more than ten yards.

Winema ground out an oath, as though he realized that in another pair of seconds Neil would come within pistol range of him. A more thoughtful man, in Winema's position, would have turned his horse and rattled away, keeping Neil at a safe distance, playing for time until he could get that carbine out and into action. Winema elected to stand his ground. He brought up his Colt's, aimed it briefly at Neil, and fired.

Neil heard the slug whine past his head. The temptation was strong in him to stop this wild downhill charge against the breed's pistol. But if he halted and posed in order to get off a shot, he would make too easy a target of himself he wouldn't live long enough to get off his shot at the gunman.

He kept on running down the slope toward Winema, who had recocked his gun and was taking deliberate, careful aim at him. Neil let out a piercing high yell, and waved his arm in an effort to spook the man's horse and spoil his aim.

The animal danced back, its eyes bugging, just as Winema pulled the trigger, and that second shot of the half-breed's was wasted.

Neil was close enough now, he decided, and he brought the muzzle of his own gun up at Winema. He had never before had occasion to shoot a pistol while running. Choosing Winema's broad chest as the best target, he pulled high, and he did not hit what he aimed at.

His first slug caught the breed in the mouth, ripping out several of the man's teeth, piercing his palate. Winema hung poised in the saddle an instant before pitching down onto the rocky underfooting in a loose-bodied, spraddle-legged dive.

His bullet-pierced head hit the stone with a sickening thud. His lax body rolled down the slope, wedging itself against the trunk of a runty jack pine.

Neil stopped running and stared at the man in a sort of weary stupor. Now that the need for violent exertion had passed, a peculiar lassitude gripped him and he couldn't bring himself to move.

Winema's horse had gone skittering off into the trees. It seemed beyond the realm of possibility to climb back up the slope to where he'd left his own horse. He sat down on an eroded smooth stone, cocking up his knees, resting his spinning head on the makeshift pillow.

He had no way of knowing how long he had been sitting there when he heard the rattle of hoofs on the sage flat below. This would be some of Frank's posse, come to find out who had been doing the shooting. His head snapped up and then a delicious sense of relief spread through him as he recognized the pair of riders down there on the flat.

They had spotted him. They came on up the slope at a run.

"Hello, Bill." Neil grinned as his redheaded foreman slid down off his horse and knelt beside him. Roy Millership was dismounting too, and Neil greeted the marshal with a weak nod. "Where'd you two come from? I was expecting some of Frank's men."

Bill Marion said gravely, "Frank's men are all with him in town, except for the one curled around the tree down the slope there." He wagged his red head from side to side, marveling at Neil. "That's a job needed doing. How'd you manage it, bunged up like you are?"

Neil told them about his fight with Winema. He asked them what Frank and his men were doing in town.

The marshal smiled. "Situation in town's not what it was last night. Frank's pulled in his horns, *and* his posses all of a sudden."

"That doesn't sound like Frank," Neil said dubiously, and again Roy Millership smiled.

"Sheriff's in town," he said. "So are John Llewellyn and most of his crew, and most of your ranching neighbors. They're plenty riled up at Frank. It's their presence in town that's makin' Frank toe the line. You can thank Ruth Orr for it."

"Ruth?" Neil said wonderingly.

Millership nodded. "She heard Frank put that five-hundred-dollar bounty on your head last night. She realized something had to be done about that, and damn sudden. She went down to the livery stable, hired a rig, and drove out to Llewellyn's place all by her lonesome to get some action out of John.

"She told him how Frank tried to buy Peyt out when he went to him begging water. John Llewellyn's no fool. It didn't take him long to figure out what Frank's up to. He sent one of his punchers back into town with Ruth, and then he started making the rounds of his neighbors. They're all in town now, fit to be tied. They've taken over the Crescent for their headquarters."

"How worked up are they?" Neil asked.

"The sheriff was doin' his best to keep the peace when me and Bill rode out here lookin' for you," said the marshal. "It's a kind of a powder-keg situation in there."

"How'd you two get together?" Neil asked. "How'd you know to look for me here?"

"I got kind of worried after you'd been gone twelve hours," Bill Marion said. "I left the boys at Stirrup to help English's crew water their beef at the lake, and rode into town. Roy, here, was with Ruth, and she gave us a list of places where we might locate you." The redhead grinned. "She says you brought her out here on a picnic years ago."

Neil nodded. Ruth had been fifteen that day, he remembered. It had been her birthday. After they'd eaten the excellent picnic lunch she'd put up for them, Neil had kissed her, for the first time.

He had a vivid memory of it, of the sweet, half-scared, but trusting way she had given her lips to him, of the warm softness of her lithe young body pressed against his. He brought himself back from daydreaming with an effort.

"I'd be dead now," he mused, "if she hadn't taken the bull by the horns and carried that news to John Llewellyn." He shook his head troubledly, adding, "I don't like that situation in town, Roy. Frank's got his back to the wall now, and his Dutch up. He'll always hit out when pressure's put on him. It's his instinct. We'd better get in there."

Millership stared at the bandaged shoulder. "Can you ride?"

Neil was thinking of Frank, thinking that the man would be dangerous as a cornered bear now. The thought of what they might find when they got into town was an increasing worry.

"I can ride," he said.

135

Chapter Eighteen

THEY RODE into town from the south, slipping unobtrusively across the railroad tracks, and picked their way along a series of garbage-strewn alleys to the rear of the Crescent.

Entering the saloon, Neil saw that nearly every outfit on the Bench was represented here, either by the ranch owner or by his foreman and a few crew members.

The bar was doing good business, judging by the rosy complexions of some of these men. Neil saw Sheriff Tobe Hendy standing alone at the bar, saw John Llewellyn sitting at a corner table with a couple of the older ranchers, and, debating briefly, he walked toward Llewellyn's table.

"What's the situation here, John?" he asked, slacking into the chair toward which the silver-haired rancher nodded.

"Still hangin' fire," said John Llewellyn, "but I don't like the looks of it. Some of these frisky young galoots are taking more whisky aboard than they know how to carry. First thing you know, one of 'em'll start something with one of Frank's men. And that's all it'll take to blow things wide open."

Neil said. "Frank and his men are upstreet in Jack's place?"

The older man nodded, and Neil looked around the room gravely. There were some fine men here in the Crescent, older men, substantial ranching men with families at home waiting for them.

"We've got to keep the lid on this thing, John," Neil said. He glanced toward the bar, and saw that Roy Millership and Bill Marion had engaged Sheriff Tobe Hendy in conversation. Eying the lawman, he frowned. "What's the sheriff been doing?"

John Llewellyn shrugged. "Standing by. Showing himself in the street every once in a while. I guess he figures his presence in town is enough to prevent the lightning from striking."

136

Neil sat rubbing his chin a moment, then said, "Excuse me, gentlemen," and went over to the bar to join Roy Millership and Bill Marion and the sheriff.

"This setup doesn't look a bit good to me, Sheriff," he murmured, taking advantage of a pause in the conversation, and the stout man looked at him and nodded.

"I don't like the looks of it either."

Neil frowned faintly. "What are you figuring to do about it?"

Hendy's eyes narrowed. "What can I do that I ain't already doing?"

"You might go up to Happy Jack's place and arrest Frank Buckmaster," Neil said quietly, and Tobe Hendy stared at him.

"Arrest him for what?"

"He raided my headquarters the other night," Neil said. "He burned down my barn."

Hendy shook his head. "Son," he said, "you know as well as I do that when ranching men take a dislike to each other and start warring, it ain't a matter for the sheriff to settle."

Neil could appreciate Hendy's viewpoint. Traditionally the cattle country settled its own quarrels. The law was not expected to take sides in a range war.

"More involved here than a fight for grass between outfits, Sheriff," Neil said. "Frank was trying to get a corner on all the dependable water around here, so he could squeeze every one else off the range."

Hendy looked at him and said, "I've heard a great deal of talk about it."

Neil frowned. "Don't you believe it?"

"As I understand it," the stout man said with an edge of irony in his voice, "English went to Frank begging water. Frank turned him down on the water, and tried to buy him out. English told you about it, you told Ruth Orr, she told John Llewellyn, and he passed the word along to the rest of these ranchers."

"And you don't believe it," Neil said.

"A man that wears a badge," Hendy said, "isn't paid to believe everything he hears. That way the jails would always be full, Ashton, at a great waste of taxpayers' money."

Neil groaned. Whether or not Hendy believed that Frank wanted Neil's water in order to whip the Bench to submission, the rest of the men in this room did believe it, and it was the liquor, steadily flowing, that made this a powder-keg situation.

Neil drew Roy Millership aside for a brief council of war. "Something's got to be done, Roy. Going to be a lot of good men killed within the next hour or so, if we don't find some way to head off the explosion."

"I been racking my brains," Millership said, "but I'm damned if I see any solution."

"Hendy's the key," Neil said. "Nobody's going to shoot a county sheriff without thinking plenty about it beforehand. We've got to nudge him down off the fence."

"How?"

Neil was silent a moment, thinking about it, and then he said, "What kind of office hours does Horace Pettingill keep, Roy?"

"Crazy. You'll generally find him open for business except when he's eating or sleeping. Why?"

"Suppose you could fetch him down here?" Neil asked, and the marshal blinked at him. "There's a question," Neil said, "that I've been wanting to ask him. It might make him a little more talkative, Roy, if you'd kind of throw a scare into him."

Millership regarded Neil for a moment, then flashed his crooked grin. "Give me five minutes," he said, and he sifted unobtrusively from the room.

When he came in again with the lawyer in tow, precisely five minutes later, it was obvious that he'd managed somehow to unnerve the lawyer. As he sidled into the room, Pettingill was cracking his knuckles at a great rate, and his face was a pasty gray.

Neil greeted Pettingill at the door with a curt nod, and then just stood staring at him in silence, sweating the man. The room had grown still, the rest of the men pausing in their talking and drinking to watch this. As the pressure piled up on Pettingill, he blurted, "What do you want of me, Ashton?"

138

"Information," Neil said. "It's been brought to my attention that you and Frank are real friendly, and there's something I'd like to know."

There was a murmur of anger from the watching men as Neil mentioned Pettingill's friendship with Frank. The lawyer's eyes bugged out behind the thick lenses of his glasses, and a fine sweat glistened on his forehead.

"I don't know what you're trying to get at," he protested.

"All I'd like to know from you," Neil said, "is how much profit was Frank going to allow you on my place, if I'd sold it to you like you suggested?"

Pettingill swallowed. "I wasn't going to make a nickel out of the transaction. I was just acting as straw man for Frank. I had no idea why he was interested in owning your outfit."

Neil only looked at the man. Pettinghill made a nervous, quick gesture with one knobby hand, and a tone of whining protest came into his voice as he said, "That's God's truth. If I'd had any notion he intended to use that water to squeeze you men out—"

The lawyer caught himself and bit at his lip, as if realizing he'd said too much. Neil turned for a questioning look at Sheriff Tobe Hendy. Pettingill, Neil suspected, had lied when he disclaimed any knowledge of Frank's plans for Stirrup, but the man's testimony could hardly help having some effect on the sheriff.

Tobe Hendy stood frowning, fingering his soft jowls. All eyes were on the lawman, and the heavy silence pressed down on the room.

"I'll need a couple of deputies," said the sheriff.

Roy Millership, looking properly grave, already was stepping forward as Neil announced quietly, "I'll go with you."

Tobe Hendy glanced at Neil's bandaged shoulder. Neil made a little gesture to indicate that it was nothing. He was thinking of the many scores he had to settle with Frank, and a grimness came into his eyes as he murmured, "I'm the logical man for this job, Sheriff."

Hendy debated a moment, then nodded. "All right." He glanced at Roy Millership, and moved deliberately toward the swing doors. Neil and the marshal followed him, and the three of them walked out of the Crescent boldly, making a display of themselves.

It was getting on toward dusk now. There was a gray remnant of daylight on the street; enough, Neil knew, to let the men down at Happy Jack's recognize them. His stomach muscles tautened a little as he followed the sheriff out onto the plank walk.

He was half expecting a fusillade from Frank and his men, but there was no shooting. A man with the sheriff in his sights thinks long and hard before pulling the trigger.

They moved deliberately along the walk. They got as far as Jack's place unchallenged. Hendy paused by the saloon's doors, pulling in a long breath. He glanced at Neil over one bulbous shoulder, whispering, "Let me talk, son," and then he pushed on into the saloon.

Frank Buckmaster, Neil saw as he entered close on the heels of the sheriff, was at the bar, flanked by a pair of his Broken Bit riders. The rest of his men were scattered about the room.

Frank had one elbow propped on the mahogany, one booted foot on the rail. There was studied casualness in the posture. This man, Neil thought, still had enormous confidence in himself, in his ability to cope with any situation.

"Hello, Tobe," Frank said. "What's on your mind?"

Hendy's glance swiveled about the big room. He spoke not to Frank, but to Frank's riders.

"I've got a word of warning for you boys. There's a situation here that could cost a lot of good men their lives, and I'm taking the only way I can see to head off trouble. I'm arresting your boss. Any man that tries to prevent me will be liable to a nice long stay in the cooler."

Frank's eyes, Neil saw, had taken on a pinched intolerance as Hendy spoke to the Broken Bit riders. And Neil tipped his hat to the stout man's shrewdness in attacking Frank obliquely, throwing a scare into Frank's men. The Broken Bit punchers were shifting uneasily, darting troubled glances at one another.

Frank saw how the sheriff's words were affecting his

140

men, and asked a blustering question: "What charge did you figure to take me on, Tobe?"

Tobe Hendy's huge head inclined toward Neil. "Ashton, here, tells me you raided his place the other night and burned down his barn, Frank."

Frank frowned. "That's nothing for you to be messing into, Tobe. That's our private squabble."

"Little more to it than that, I'm beginning to realize," Tobe Hendy said dryly. "Better come along, Frank."

"Now wait a minute—" Frank said, but Tobe Hendy cut him off, saying, "I'm taking you in, Frank."

Neil saw the first faint suggestion of fear touch the big man's eyes then. Tobe Hendy's tone had said he was not fooling, and Neil, sensing the climactic moment, sent his glance flicking about the room, watching Frank's men, ready to draw and shoot the instant any of them made a gesture toward a weapon.

Roy Millership, Neil saw out of the corner of one eye, was also poised for action, backing up the sheriff's play.

The seconds raveled on, and Frank stood there. He had a cigar in his hand. He stuck it in his mouth and drew on it, but it had gone dead. He looked down at it, frowning at it, as if debating whether to throw it away or relight it.

He leaned forward with the apparent intention of dropping the cigar into a cuspidor, and curled his left arm around the neck of the puncher standing beside him. He pulled the man back against him, using the fellow's body as a shield for his own.

With his right hand he whipped out his gun, and shot at Tobe Hendy.

The stout man grunted and went down, his gun flashing. The man Frank was holding against him let out a scream of pain, which Frank disregarded.

The instant Neil saw what Frank's game was, he dropped to one knee and brought up his gun. He saw one of Frank's men whip out his gun, and shot the man down, and then somebody put a bullet into the overhead lamp, and the room darkened abruptly.

Neil lay prone on the floor. Several of Frank's men were shooting, their lead whipping over his head. He shouted,

"You damn fools, you'll all swing if Frank's killed the sheriff!" The shooting stopped. There was the sound of a door opening and closing at the rear of the room.

A voice said in the darkness, "Frank?" and another voice said disgustedly, "He's flew the coop. He's left us holdin' the bag here."

Neil knew then that there was nothing more to be feared from Frank's riders. He rose and stepped out deliberately through the saloon's bat-wing doors, pinning himself for a moment against the front of the building, in the awning's black shadow.

There were no horses racked out there in front of the saloon. It occurred to him that Frank, having callously sacrificed one of his crewmen in order to make good his escape, had alienated his riders, and was, in effect, alone in a hostile town now.

How do *you* like it, Frank? Neil wondered.

Frank and his men had put up their horses at Piperock's stables, and there was always the possibility that Frank, with that panicky fear of the hunted animal driving him, would show up there.

Neil hurried down Main Street, hugging the darkness in front of the buildings. He turned in through the stable's high arch. The tiny cubicle that served the attendant as an office was deserted.

Apparently the groom had gone into hiding, along with the rest of Piperock's peaceful citizens, and Neil smiled grimly as he moved along the packed-earth runway toward the rear of the stable's manure-littered yard, where a gate in the seven-foot fence provided a rear entrance.

He posted himself by the stable building, standing in shadow under wide eaves. He was only thirty feet from the fence gate, and he eased his gun in the leather and waited.

Nothing happened. There was no sound or movement to disturb the night's quiet, and as the minutes went by he felt a wicked impatience.

He was telling himself that he had guessed wrong, that Frank was not going to come, when he saw the gate latch rise slowly.

Somebody on the other side of the gate was levering

142

the latch to disengage it. The gate moved on its hinges, creaking a little. It opened just enough to permit Frank Buckmaster to ease his huge body through.

Frank didn't bother to close the gate. He started along the runway toward the stable office. Moonlight was on him. The light strengthened briefly, and Neil saw something in Frank's face that surprised him.

Supreme self-assurance was gone, and in its place was the taut, twisted expression of a hunted man. He's scared, Neil thought, marveling. He's been a bully all his life, and now, for the first time, he's finding out what it feels like to be scared.

There was an urgency in Frank's stride, in his every gesture. The big man had not seen Neil, standing there against the wall of the stable.

Neil said, "Going someplace, Frank?" and saw stiffness come to Frank's body.

The big man halted and pivoted slowly. His glance flicked along the stable wall until he picked Neil out. He stood there regarding Neil for a moment, a man accustomed to having his way, not having it this night.

Neil had waited for this moment. He stepped out of the stable's shadow, letting Frank see him. His gun was in his hand, leveled at Frank, and now, as Frank stared at him, he deliberately holstered the weapon.

"All right, Frank," he said softly, and he watched the big man, waiting for Frank to make a gesture at his own weapon. Frank didn't move. He seemed unable to bring himself to action, and Neil said, "Have a try, Frank. You'll hang anyway, if you killed the sheriff."

Frank refused to be baited. He said quietly, speaking past Neil, "Let him have it, Johnny."

Neil laughed. "Winema's dead, Frank. I'd know, inasmuch as I shot him."

Frank growled and started toward Neil, lowering his hand to his gun. He shot swiftly, angrily, the slug tugging at Neil's shirt, spoiling Neil's own shot.

There was a kind of wildness in Frank now that set his eyes aglow in the moonlight, that pulled his lips away from his teeth.

Frank palm-cocked, and was shooting again as Neil's

143

second shot found the target. The big man grunted and stepped back. Neil was still standing, unhit, and now Frank used both hands in a terrible effort to recock his gun.

He was trying to lift the muzzle of the weapon when Neil shot him again. The slug hammered Frank back. His tripping, back-pedaling feet couldn't keep pace with his upper body. He fell, hitting the manure-littered ground with a jarring thump.

Frank's gun had dropped from his hand, and lay several yards from him. Neil went over and bent to pick up the weapon. He was standing there staring down at Frank's lifeless body when John Llewellyn came jogging in off the street, followed by a group of Neil's ranching neighbors.

John Llewellyn looked down at Frank's inert figure and said soberly, "Son, it appears we're all in your debt."

Neil saw Roy Millership hurrying in from the street, and called to him, "What about the sheriff?"

"Frank got him through the fatty part of the leg. He's sitting up, cussing like a mule skinner." Millership sobered. "Frank's crew will skip out. They'll be poison on this range now, and they know it."

It was over, Neil realized. A weariness almost of the soul wafted through him. He walked out to the street, turning along it toward Third Street, toward Ruth's place.

He found her sitting on the porch in the dark, and told her what had happened. "I'm a Bench rancher now, Ruth, in good standing. It's what I've wanted, but it doesn't mean much." He hesitated. "I'm beginning to find out that nothing in this life does, unless you have someone to share things with."

He reached down, taking her by one slender wrist, lifting her gently. She hesitated only an instant, and rose from the chair.

"You were right," she murmured, "when you said I'm not fickle. It's always been you, Neil, even when I was trying to convince myself I'd got you out of my system."

She was against him then, her body warm, her lips willing.